# PARLOR GAMES

---

## AN EROTIC ADVENTURE

### VICTORIA RUSH

# VOLUME 27

JADE'S EROTIC ADVENTURES - BOOK 27

# COPYRIGHT

**FEEL THE RUSH:**

**Jade's Erotic Adventures – Book 1**

*When lonely divorcée Jade seeks to broaden her horizons, she's invited to a private dinner event which promises to stimulate all of her senses. Wearing nothing but masquerade masks, dinner guests receive special service under the table while their fellow diners look on...*

The Dinner Party

**Jade's Erotic Adventures - Book 2**

*Jade discovers an exotic adventure club where strangers meet to explore each other's bodies in mysterious dark rooms. Using special effects to project swirling light patterns onto their figures, the shifting shadows provide just enough illumination to highlight their naked bodies while protecting their identities...*

The Dark Room

**Jade's Erotic Adventures - Book 3**

*Jade discovers a yoga club where members stretch and explore each other's bodies in the buff. She books an appointment, and during the first session meets a young redhead who tantalizes her with her flexibility and stunning body...*

Naked Yoga

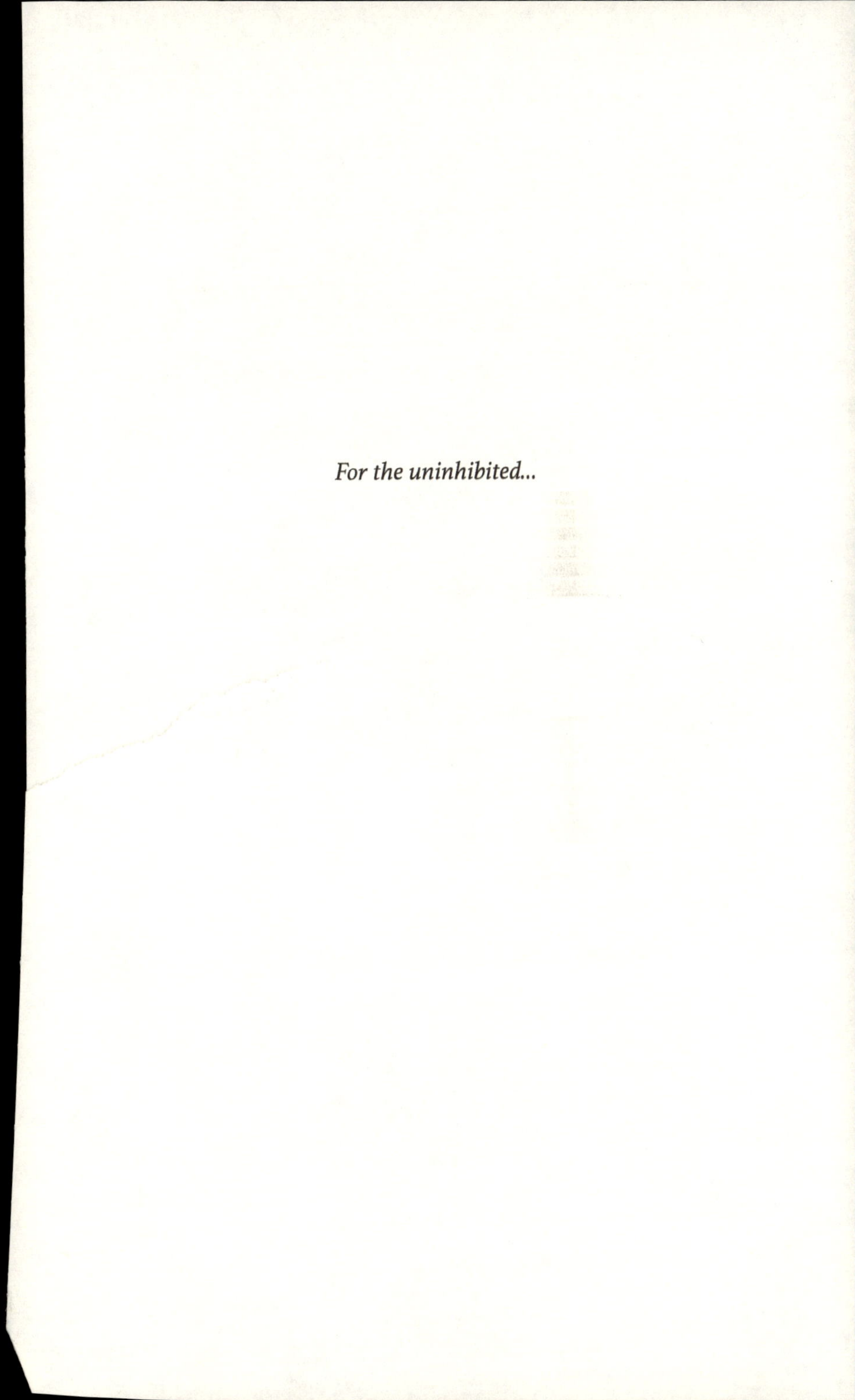

*For the uninhibited...*

1
─────

## THE INVITATION

This had to be the strangest party invitation I'd ever received.

And the most titillating.

It was from my friend Madison, and the subject heading simply read *Parlor Game*:

*You are cordially invited to a special party at Madison's house, Saturday, June 15, at 9:00 p.m. sharp. Dress code is optional. It's a sit-down affair, but I assure you it will be anything but boring. Be prepared to be entertained like you've never been before. Come alone, but come often!*

*Mad*

*P.S.: There will be special arrival procedures. Text me five minutes before you get to the door. Please be punctual because the game cannot be interrupted once started. RSVP by Friday, 6:00 p.m.*

WTF? I thought upon first reading the invitation. *What kind of parlor game is 'dress code optional'? Did that mean we were free to wear whatever we wanted, or did it mean we were meant to wear no clothing at all? And why couldn't I bring a date?*

But I liked the *come often* idea.

*What was Madison up to this time?* I knew she had a kinky side, but I had no idea what she had planned for this event. Who could turn down such an invitation? Her parties always had the most interesting people, the best music, and plenty of unexpected hook-ups.

I picked up the phone and called her as soon as I got the message, dying to get all the dirt on this shindig.

"Whassup, gurl?" Maddie said when she answered my call, recognizing my caller ID.

"You've definitely got my attention now," I said.

"You got my message?"

"Uh–*yeah*. That is one crazy, cryptic invite. What are you getting us into this time?"

"Sorry, I can't provide any more details," she said. "Need to know only. Everything will be explained when you arrive. Are you coming?"

"How could I *not*, with that kind of invitation? But I'm confused about your dress code comment. I have no idea what to wear."

"It doesn't matter what you wear. I assure you no one will be paying attention to any of that."

"Oh, *come on!*" I said. "Now you've really got me squirming in my chair. You have to give me at least a *hint* at what's going to happen. Is it at least *legal*?"

"Of course," she said. "We're all consenting adults. But there will be an opt-out clause for anyone who doesn't feel comfortable participating. I'd never put my friends in a compromising position."

"Okay, you've twisted my arm," I said. "But what's this

calling five minutes ahead business? I've never heard of such a thing beyond the usual RSVP."

"It's just to ensure the privacy and confidentiality of our guests. It's the anonymity of the affair that makes this party so special."

*Anonymity?* I thought. *So I'm not going to know anyone who'll be attending? How does she propose to maintain everyone's privacy?* This thing was getting weirder and more exciting by the moment.

"Fine," I said, shaking my head in frustration. "Your house, your rules. But this better be everything it's cracked up to be. Because now you've seriously raised my expectations."

"I hope that's not the *only* thing I've raised," she purred over the phone. "See you Saturday at nine. Don't be late!"

When I hung up the phone, I could feel my heart pounding in my chest. The call had done nothing to lessen my confusion about the event, only to further arouse my curiosity and excitement. And yes, she'd definitely succeeded in raising more than just my expectations. Feeling my clit hardening in my panties, I opened my blouse and squeezed my erect nipples.

I wasn't sure what I was getting myself into, but my rapidly moistening panties told me this wasn't going to be a party soon forgotten.

## 2

## IN THE DARK

On the night of the event, I circled Madison's block at least three times trying to get a better idea about this mysterious game she'd cooked up. But all I could see was a slow procession of strangers approaching her door, one at a time. In each case, she opened the door to greet them, then closed it just as quickly. I had no way of determining how many guests had arrived or what was going on inside. I thought I recognized a few cars parked on the adjoining streets, but there was no way of knowing for sure if they belonged to people I knew.

*Note to self. Next time take a pic of my friend's plate and attach it to their contact listing on my phone. You never know when that might come in handy.*

On my fourth go-round, I called Maddie from the next street over five minutes before nine. I didn't want to be the first one to break protocol and miss any of the fun.

"I'm here," I said when I heard her pick up.

"Cool," she said. "Find a parking spot close to the house, then come up to the door in five minutes. I'll greet you and get you all set up."

*Set up?* I thought, hanging up the phone. *What does that mean? And what's with all this careful spacing of guests? Isn't a party supposed to be all about getting to know one another and meeting new faces?*

No matter, I thought, circling around the block and finding a spot on the side of her street four houses down. Judging by the number of cars queued up, it looked like it was going to be an intimate affair. I walked up to her door and tapped the bell. Madison opened the door and after glancing outside to make sure I was alone, she ushered me into her foyer.

"Glad you could make it," she said, smiling at me. "I was afraid I might have scared you off."

"Are you kidding me?" I said. "Wild horses couldn't keep me from coming to this party. If only to see what you've got cooked up."

"I'm glad," she said. "It wouldn't be the same without you."

She pulled a thin black cloth out of a bag resting on the floor and handed it to me. "First up, I need you to put this on."

"A *blindfold*?" I said, widening my eyes. "What for?"

"You'll see," she said. "Maybe not in the *literal* sense, but everything will become apparent soon enough."

She carefully positioned the bandana over my eyes then tied it firmly behind my head.

"No peeking," she said. "That'll ruin all the fun. Not to mention everyone's privacy."

"I couldn't even if I wanted to," I said, feeling the soft fabric wrap snugly over my nose and cheekbones, blocking out my entire field of vision. "Are you going to escort me inside so I don't break a leg?"

"Of course. But you'll have to strip first."

"Say *what*?" I said, cocking my head.

"Oh *please*," she said. "You've never been shy about showing off your amazing body before."

"Well yes, but that was usually with a modicum of cover or around people I know. In this case, I have no idea who'll I be exposing myself to."

"Nor will they. That's why everybody *else* will be blind-folded too."

"Okay," I said, beginning to understand why she'd been so careful not to let anyone see her arriving guests. "But is it safe? I mean, how do I know I'm not going to be accosted by some stranger once I get to the meeting room?"

"You've got nothing to worry about. Everyone will be seated two feet apart on separate chairs. And remember, you can always pull out anytime you feel uncomfortable. I've got your back, girl."

"Jesus, Mad," I sighed. "You are one twisted bitch. I'm just going to have to trust that you know what you're doing."

I started removing my clothes and handed them to Madison and when I was completely naked, she escorted me down a hall into another room where I heard her place my belongings on a table. Then she took my hand and led to me to terrycloth towel-covered chair and eased me down onto it.

"I'll be back after the next guest arrives," she said. "You're welcome to chat with the other guests already here while I'm away. Just don't reveal any names and keep your blind-fold in place to maintain the secrecy. The party will get started shortly."

I heard Madison head back to the foyer then for the next few awkward moments, silence filled the room.

"Welcome, new guest," a baritone man's voice said.

I couldn't place him, but he sounded about my age, mid-thirties.

Okay, so at least I know it's a *co-ed* affair.

"Hello," I said timidly, placing my right leg overtop of my knee to protect my modesty.

"It's okay," a woman's voice said. "We were just as freaked out when we got here too."

"Good to know," I nodded, happy to hear another woman's voice in the crowd. The idea of sitting stark naked in a room full of naked strangers was disconcerting to say the least, but strangely arousing. I shifted uncomfortably in my chair, hearing the sound of plastic squeaking underneath me.

"That's a voice I recognize," a familiar-sounding woman said.

It sounded like my friend Lily from last year's camping trip. We'd shared a brief but passionate fling on our one-week excursion into the woods of northern Canada, and suddenly I felt the space between my overlapping thighs become slippery with lubrication.

"Is that–?"

"Sh!" she quickly interrupted me. "No names, remember? You don't want to get kicked out before all the fun starts."

"Mmm," I nodded, squeezing my thighs even tighter together, feeling my clit twitching in excitement between my legs.

I could hear the sound of another guest arriving and quiet murmuring from the other end of the house, then Madison escorted the person into the room and sat him down with the rest of the group. From the minimal smalltalk we'd engaged in during her absence, it sounded like everyone was arranged in a circle roughly twenty feet in diameter. I smiled at Madison's ingenuity concocting such a bold idea, and as I listened to the group of strangers talking around me, my mind began to wander with what she intended to do with us.

When the last guest was seated, I heard her take a seat a few feet to my left as she opened the proceedings.

"First off," she said. "I want to thank everyone for coming. I know it was a pretty vague invitation, and I can't blame any of you if you're wondering what you've gotten yourself into. But I know each of you well enough to know that you're open to new adventures and that you're reasonably uninhibited, if that's the right word."

"If we weren't before, we sure as hell are *now*," the husky-voiced man said.

Everybody chuckled nervously, then Madison continued her briefing.

"Okay, I won't keep you in suspense any longer. What I had in mind was a kind of free association body exploration between willing partners. I thought it might be kind of fun to receive, and then later on, provide some physical stimulation to a chosen partner one at a time, without anyone actually knowing who was doing the giving and who was receiving the stimulation..."

"And by *stimulation* you mean–" I heard Lily enquire.

"Whatever your partner feels comfortable providing. And what you feel comfortable receiving. Because of the blindfolds and the no-name rule, each of the connections will be anonymous. I'll make the initial introductions, and then it's up to each couple to decide how far they wish to proceed. In some cases, you'll be able to guess the gender of your partner, and in some cases you may not. But in all cases, you won't know who it is you're engaging with.

"Unless, that is," Madison said. "You have a prior history

with that person and you're specially attuned to your partner's technique and endowments."

"What about–?" someone said, voicing what all of us were thinking.

"For heterosexual combinations, I've put aside a set of condoms on each of your tables to your right. Along with your choice of beer, wine, or cocktails in unspillable containers. Sorry for the sippy cups, but I thought some of you might need a little extra lubrication to get started, and we don't want to make too much of a mess."

"Speaking of–" another woman said.

"You'll also find a tube of lube on each of your tables, should you feel the need. As for cleanliness and diseases, each of you is on your honor to step away or refuse to participate if you have any known issues."

Awkward silence suddenly filled the room.

"Is there some kind of *goal* or *prize* with this parlor game?" I asked. "Or are we just supposed to go with the flow and take everything it as it comes?"

"There will be special prizes later on in the evening for each partner who correctly guesses who received and who provided stimulation. But I suspect the main reward will be enjoyed while you're *living* the experience."

I could hear nervous laughter around the circle as everyone knew exactly what Madison meant.

"Okay," she said. "Now that you understand the rules of engagement, anyone is free to withdraw if you're feeling at all uncomfortable, or abstain from participating once given the choice. I've assembled a small enough group that everyone should have a chance both to receive and give before the evening is over. Does anybody want out?"

Awkward silence filled the room again as I listened to the sound of guests shifting uncomfortably in their chairs.

Whether it was because they were nervous or because they were already becoming aroused, I couldn't be sure, but I certainly knew which it was in *my* case.

"Okay then," Madison said. "Let the fun begin. Raise your hand if you want to be the first to give it a try."

I heard the sound of shifting a few chairs away, but I decided to hold back to see how things played out at first.

"Good," Madison said. "I see some of you guys came to play. We've got our first two candidates."

I heard Madison rise from her chair and walk to the other side of the circle, then a pair of footfalls approached a chair a few feet to my right.

"You may proceed at your leisure," Madison said. "If at any time you feel uncomfortable or wish to stop the engagement, simply cross your arms and/or legs and your partner will stop immediately. However, if you're enjoying what you're experiencing, I encourage each of you to let down your guard as much as you feel comfortable and open yourself up to all the possibilities."

"Can we *talk* to our partner while we're engaged in the process?" a man's voice said in front of the chair.

"By all means," Madison said. "Feel free to provide whatever guidance, requests or feedback you feel heightens the experience. The only rule is no revealing of names, and no peeking at any time."

As I listened to the sound of the man kneeling on the carpet in front of the chair, I placed my hands in my lap and pressed my fingers down over the front of my mound. Even before I'd been touched by anyone, I was already feeling more excited and aroused than I'd been in a long time.

3

______

**MF**

For the first couple of minutes, I could only hear the sound of the man's hands caressing someone's skin and the subtle squeaking of a chair to my right. I didn't even know if it was a man or a woman who he'd been paired with, and my mind raced with the idea of stretching each of our sexual boundaries. Although I considered myself pansexual, I suspected many of the other guests considered themselves straight who wouldn't under normal circumstances engage in intimate relations with another person of the same sex.

But this was far from typical circumstances. Madison had created a unique, non-judgmental environment for open-minded strangers to explore each other's bodies while focusing only on the sensations they were giving and receiving. It was a brilliant idea, and I could feel the terrycloth towel under my butt already moistening from the stream of juices beginning to run down my vulva. Now I knew why she'd covered each of the chairs with a plastic screen and a towel. I was pretty sure I wasn't the *only* one getting this turned on listening to the two strangers exploring each other's bodies in the dark.

Suddenly, I heard a woman moaning where the man had been placed, and the sound of plastic squeaking under her seat.

*Okay,* I thought. *So this first pairing is a man giving pleasure to a woman. Madison's playing it safe to start, hoping to ease everybody's nervousness about engaging with an unidentified stranger.* Although I preferred lesbian sex myself, I was not above enjoying other people's intimate relations, especially at a safe distance.

"Mmm," I heard the woman purr, squeaking her chair more loudly.

It was obvious to all of us that whatever the man was doing, she was enjoying his attention while she squirmed her hips on the chair.

"That feels good," she said, encouraging him to continue. "I want to feel your hands on my breasts. Squeeze my tits and pinch my nipples."

"Hmm," the man hummed in acknowledgment, shifting his position closer to her body on the plush carpet below my feet.

"Yes," she hissed, feeling the man's hands caressing her tits. "Whoever you are, I like your touch. Now suck my nipples while I run my fingers through your hair..."

I heard the sound of wet lips smacking on skin as the woman groaned, and I spread my knees apart, circling my clit listening to her getting more and more turned on by the man's ministrations. There was something incredibly sexy about not knowing who was engaged in the veiled sex act or what they looked like.

While the smacking and moaning sounds continued a few chairs away, I began to hear the squeaking of chairs and subtle sighs of *other* people around the circle. It was obvious that many of the other attending guests had become just as aroused as I was from what was going on beside them, and they felt brave enough to touch themselves knowing nobody else was watching.

*Nobody except Madison,* I smiled. *You scheming bitch. You designed this scenario not only for the enjoyment of your guests, but so you could shamelessly watch everybody while they pleasured one another and themselves.* I could only imagine what she was doing while this was all going down. It must have been a feast for her eyes watching the naked couple exploring each other's bodies, not to mention all the guests touching themselves while they listened in.

"Can you feel how hard my nipples are getting?" the woman said as the man continued sucking her teats.

"Oh yes," the man murmured with his face buried in her cleavage.

"Start licking your way down the front of my stomach. There's something *else* getting hard that needs your attention."

"Mmm," the man purred, kneeling back on the carpet as he lowered his face down her body.

"Yes," she moaned. "Just like that. Rub your rough face over my bare mound. I want to feel your stubble scratching my skin before you fuck me."

*Jesus,* I thought, spreading my legs further apart while I jilled my clit furiously. I could feel the towel underneath me getting wetter by the moment as I listened to these two strangers ramping up the action. There was a whole extra level of excitement from not being able to see what was going on and only being able to listen to the two lovers as they touched one another. It was true what they said about our other senses being heightened when another one is compromised. My whole body was buzzing like it had an electric current running through it.

I could hear the scratching sound of the man's whiskers rubbing against the woman's skin, and knowing how close his face was to her most sensitive part was driving me crazy with anticipation. And from the sound of the rustling plastic all around me, apparently I wasn't the only one who felt this way.

"Now put your face between my legs and lick my lips up and down," the woman instructed. "I want you to taste my juices while I feel your bristles between my legs."

*Holy shit*, I thought, placing my palm over my snatch, rubbing my entire vulva with my hand. *I love the way she's bossing him around like he's her slave. It must be driving him crazy not being able to be touched himself. Kind of like the rest of us, except we've got a little more freedom of expression not having other distractions getting in the way.*

"Fuck, yes," the woman groaned. "Your tongue feels so warm on my lips. Now stick it inside me and fuck me while I pull your face into my crotch."

I could hear the sound of wet skin slapping against each other as other voices around the room began to moan and sigh in concert with the woman next to me. Imagining it was me on the receiving end of the man's attention, I stuck my middle finger in my pussy and began fucking myself while I circled my nub with my other hand.

"Deeper," the woman moaned. "I want to feel you probing into my deepest recesses. You're sucking my cunny like a good boy."

"Um-hmm," the man hummed, obviously enjoying the feedback he was getting from his partner while he ate her pussy.

As I listened to the muffled sound of his voice, I imagined her grabbing the back of his hair while she held his face against her cunt. I placed both of my hands between my legs and closed my thighs around them, envisioning it was the man's head pressed against my sex instead of my hands. I could feel my pleasure beginning to rise, but I wanted to hold off coming so I could enjoy the woman's orgasm fully.

"That's it, baby," she growled. "Fuck my pussy with your tongue. I'm getting close now. Lift your head and take my button into your mouth. Suck my clit like you've never sucked on anything before. Make me cum all over your face."

"If you insist," the man murmured with gentle laughter filling the room.

This whole experience was turning out to be even more exciting than I had envisioned. Multi-gender partner swapping with the mystery of not being able to see the couples in action, and even a little humor.

*I have got to try this blindfold thing with more of my own partners,* I thought. *What a great way to get more attuned to their touch and learn to give better feedback.*

Suddenly, the woman gasped as the plastic on her chair squeaked from the shifting of her ass on the seat. There wasn't much mystery as to what they were doing to each other now. As the licking sounds escalated in volume along with the movement of her hips in her chair, everybody knew he was now sucking on her clit while she pressed his face between her legs.

"Yes," she panted. "Suck my bean and swirl your tongue over it like you're licking a lollypop. I'm going to come in your mouth soon."

"Mmm," the man hummed in assent, not wanting to interrupt the rhythm of his tongue action.

I could only imagine how hard he must have been

kneeling between her legs as he sucked her pussy, listening to the sound of her escalating tension. I could almost *see* the cum dripping from the tip of his penis onto the carpet below her chair while he focused on maximizing her pleasure. I nodded at how clever Madison had been in separating the acts of giving and receiving so that each person could enjoy the experience to the fullest without any other distraction.

"That's it, baby," the woman grunted. "Suck me harder. I'm going to come any second."

As I listened to the sound of the woman's chair squeaking and her breath rising in pitch, I spread my legs further apart and pinched my clit between my fingers while I rubbed it up and down. I was ready to come along with the woman, and there was no longer anything holding me back from expressing myself fully. I didn't care if my seatmates heard what I was doing or how much pleasure I was giving myself. This blind exploration experience had turned out to be more arousing than any explicit porno I'd watched on my computer on lonely nights.

"Yes!" the woman grunted. "Don't stop. Oh God, I'm going to cum! I'm gonna cum so hard in your mouth. *Fuckkk!*"

As I listened to the woman wailing at the top of her lungs, I felt my own orgasm wash over me while I clamped my legs together and gushed all over my hands. After my climax began to ebb, I became more aware of the sounds of the other people in the room as they experienced their own climaxes listening to the sexy couple. With everybody grunting and gasping in collective ecstasy, I turned my head to face Madison, knowing she was watching the whole scene only a few chairs away.

*You little fucker,* I smiled. *You knew exactly what you were getting us into.* I was so turned on I wanted to jump out of my chair and grind my pussy against her face just like the woman had done with the man.

But I knew that would have to wait. There were still too many *other* possibilities to explore in the meantime.

After a few moments, I heard the sound of the woman's breathing return to normal and the man pull away, wondering what to do next. Although she'd just had a powerful orgasm, there were still many other ways they could connect, and he must have been bursting in anticipation. Sensing his discomfort, the woman sat up in her chair and cleared her throat.

"God damn," she said. "You sure know how to satisfy a woman with your mouth. Can I see what *else* you've got to work with?"

I heard the man rise up from his kneeling position and take a step forward. I could imagine his hard pole dripping in anticipation as he pressed it closer to her face, when Madison, who'd been silent up to now, suddenly interrupted their proceedings.

"Remember the rules," she said. "Each interaction is limited to giving or receiving only. The gentleman will have his opportunity to receive equivalent attention in due course. You can't touch him sexually yet–only *he* can touch *you.*"

"That hardly seems fair," the woman huffed. "I'm dying to feel the rest of his package. Can't he touch me with his *cock* also?"

"If that's what you'd like," Madison said. "You just can't touch him in return. At least not *that* way."

"So *other* parts of my body are allowed to touch him, as long as he's taking the lead?"

"Um-hmm," Madison nodded.

"You heard the lady," the woman snarled, shifting her weight in her chair. "Assume the position. I'm ready to feel something *else* in my pussy now."

"If you insist," the man said as the rest of the room chuckled softly.

"But go slow," the woman instructed. "Since I can't touch you with my hands, I want to savor every inch of your cock as you slide inside me. Lift my legs over my shoulders and point your python into my hole."

I heard the sound of the plastic squeaking loudly, then the chair creaked as the woman's weight shifted further back toward her backrest.

"Yes, baby," she purred. "I'm so wet for you. Let me feel the head of your cock pressing into my cunt. Let's savor this moment together."

With the sound of her dirty talk getting me all worked up again, I lifted my feet on top of my chair seat, spreading my knees far apart like I imagined hers were. Suddenly I wished I'd had the foresight to bring one of my favorite dildos to fuck myself at this moment, but I wasn't sure that would be allowed under Madison's rules. Then I remembered that she said each of us had a tube of lube next to us on our side tables. Desperate for anything to put inside me, I reached over and tapped the table gently until I felt a cylinder-shaped object.

*Thank God*, I thought, running my fingers over the round cap and the tapered end of the tube. *This stuff is going to come in handy in more ways than one.* I picked up the tube and placed the round end against my hole, half expecting her to stop me. Fortunately, her attention seemed to be directed elsewhere, and I groaned as I pressed the tube into my slit.

"Do you need me to–?" the man said, remembering the instructions Madison had given us earlier regarding protection.

"It's already taken care of," the woman purred. "I want to feel your bare skin inside me. I've got my *own* protection."

The man exhaled heavily. I wasn't sure if it was from relief at not having to worry about fumbling with a condom or because he'd reached the limit of his self-control. He lifted the woman's thighs up toward her chest and took a step closer to her. Suddenly both of them groaned as they joined in congress.

"Fuck yes," the woman moaned. "Your dick is so warm. And *thick*. Tease me with your head while I imagine how much more you've got to give me."

The chair began to squeak softly as the man shifted his weight back and forth, lubricating the head of his cock with her juices.

"Mmm," the woman said. "That feels good. "Is it good for you too?"

"Uh-huh," the man grunted.

For a brief moment, I considered lifting my blindfold just enough to see his pole probing her slit, but I dared not be the first to break Madison's rules. I didn't want to inter-rupt their rhythm with another reprimand from my friend. And besides, she'd put so much forethought and planning into this event, it would be unfair to spoil the fun.

"Okay," the woman continued. "Now slowly push your dick further inside me so I can feel every inch of your burning meat. I want to feel you impale me all the way to the hilt."

"Uhnn," the man groaned as he pressed himself further into her hole.

"God damn," the woman purred. "That's one hell of a joystick. I can feel you spreading me apart the further you go inside me."

"Yes," the man grunted. "You're so tight and wet. Squeeze me while I give you all eight inches."

I heard a few gasps around the room, and smiled imagining how turned on many of the women and some of the men were imagining themselves on the receiving end of his snake.

"Oh God," the woman groaned, feeling him press more and more of his length inside her. "Fill me up, baby. Let me feel all of you inside me now. I want you to pound your meat inside my pussy."

The man grunted as he thrust his full weight against her splayed legs, and she shuddered when he reached the end of her tunnel.

"Holy shit!" she gasped. "You weren't kidding about the size of your cock. I can feel you pressing up against my uterus. Be careful you don't slam me too hard. You might *kill* me with that thing."

"No worries," he said. "I'll be careful. Just let me know if I'm hurting you."

"Ahh," a few women muttered around the room, apparently equally taken by his sexiness as by his concern for his partner.

I pressed the tube of lube as far into my hole as I dared, gripping the tapered end tightly with the fingers of my right hand. The last thing I needed was to lose it inside my pussy and have to go to the hospital to have it removed. Besides, I had *other* purposes I was saving my pussy for. I needed to keep it unoccupied in case Madison decided to hook me up with a man later.

It didn't take long for me to hear the unmistakable sound of the man's penis thrusting in and out of her pussy as their wet bellies slapped together and the woman's chair squeaked loudly next to me.

"Fuck yes," the woman grunted. "Fuck me with that spear. You feel so good. I want to feel you shooting your load inside my pussy."

"Uhnn, uhnn, uhnn," the man groaned as he slammed his cock in and out of her hole. I could hear the sound of his balls flapping against the underside of her vulva as the sloshing sound of her dripping pussy filled the room.

But that wasn't the *only* thing I heard in the room. From almost every direction around the circle, I could hear the grunting and moaning sounds of both men and women pleasuring themselves as they listened to the couple copulating only a few feet away.

I pulled the tube out of my pussy for a moment, then flipped open the cap and squeezed a dollop of lube inside my hole. Then I closed the lid and thrust it back inside me while I trilled my fingers over my burning clit.

"Yes, baby," the woman panted. "I want to feel you come inside me. I'm getting close–"

"Ahem," Madison suddenly interrupted again. "I hate to disturb your fun at this delicate moment. But I want to remind both of you of the rules. Remember, this engagement is designed for the *woman's* pleasure only. Unfortunately, I must ask the gentleman to resist the temptation to consummate the act. Your focus must be on *giving* pleasure for the moment, not receiving."

"Argh," I heard the man groan in frustration.

"Are you *kidding* me?" the woman complained. "If the goal is to give me pleasure, nothing would make me happier

than to have my partner experience the penultimate pleasure along with me."

"That may be true," Madison said. "But he'll have to wait
his turn. That's the main attraction, focusing on *one* person's
pleasure at a time. If you break the rules, I'm going to have
to ask each of you to sit out the rest of the proceedings in a
passive role."

"Alright Tiger," the woman said, readjusting her position
in her chair. "I'm close. Do you think you can hold off long
enough until I climax?"

"I'll try," he said. "Maybe if you take over more of the
rocking action. The harder I thrust inside you, the harder it
will be not to come."

"Okay," she said. "Just hold steady while I do all the work.
Pretend you're a rock while I fuck your magnificent penis.
Someone *else* is going to have a wonderful awakening later
this evening when they take matters into their own hands."

I heard the woman grip the arms of her chair and begin
to rock her hips forward and back as the plastic squeezed
under her ass while she fucked the man's pole with her slippery pussy.

"I'm fucking you baby," she panted. "I'm fucking your
red-hot poker with my dripping cunt. I'm going to come all
over your balls. Are you ready?"

"Uhhh," the man groaned, straining with all his might to
resist popping off inside her.

"Here it comes baby," she said. "I'm going to cum all over
your big firehose. Oh! Oh! *Uhhhn!*"

As I listened to the sound of the woman grunting in the
throes of another orgasm, I pulled my knees together and
clamped down over the tube of lube planted inside my
pussy while I hissed in ecstasy from the feeling of my own
orgasm taking hold of me. This time, there was less reluc-

tance on the part of the rest of the crowd to hold back as they grunted and groaned in orgasmic unison with the woman a few seats over.

While I rocked forward and back in my seat with my entire body quivering in excitement, I couldn't help thinking about the man who'd been forced to contain his pleasure while she rolled her flapping pussy over his giant organ. With any luck, I thought, I'll be the one to finish him off later this evening. I was already beginning to think about how I could make it up to him.

**4**

———

**FF**

For a few moments after the woman came, the only thing I could hear in the room was the sound of other people shuffling in their seats and towels rubbing up against bare skin. It was obvious that I wasn't the only one who'd made a mess cumming so hard listening to the sexy man and woman next to me. I envied Madison being able to spy on everybody pleasuring themselves while each couple engaged in their own sexual exploration. It was a brilliant idea on so many levels, and I resolved to hold my *own* blindfold party at the first opportunity.

"So what happens now?" the woman next to me said after she recovered from her orgasm. "My partner is still hard, and I can think of many other ways he can still satisfy me."

"I'm sure he could," Madison said. "But I think it's time to let some of our other guests share in the fun."

*As if they haven't already,* I grinned under my blindfold as I wiped the dripping tube of lube off with the towel under my seat and placed it back on the table next to me. It felt strangely liberating being able to touch myself with my body on full display, knowing that nobody could actually see me.

"If the gentleman could, um, *extricate* himself now and take his seat," Madison said, seeing the man's cock still impaled in the woman's pussy. "I'd like to ask for a new set of volunteers to continue the entertainment."

I heard the sudden squeaking of plastic all around the circle as everyone threw up their hand.

"Whoa!" Madison exclaimed. "We can't take everybody at once. What do you say we mix it up a little bit this time? If you guys are game to try something a little different, I've got a couple of candidates in mind."

I could almost picture everyone's head nodding as they begged to be chosen next. But knowing Maddie, I knew she'd want to stretch the next couple's boundaries.

"Okay," she said, walking to the other side of the circle. "I think I've identified another interesting pairing. Let me take your hand and escort you to your next partner."

I heard a pair of footfalls crunch across the plush carpet to the opposite side of my circle, three or four chairs away.

"I'll leave you now in the capable hands of your partner," Madison said. "But remember the rules. Only one person at a time can enjoy each coupling. Like the gentleman before, one of you will have to save yourself to receive similar attention later in the evening. Are you guys ready to resume the festivities?"

I heard the shifting of a body in the chair to my left, then the sound of someone kneeling on the carpet in front of the chair. I smiled at how tentative each of the partners were in beginning each engagement, first wanting to identify the other person's sex before deciding to become more actively involved. I still had no idea who'd been paired together, and my pussy throbbed in anticipation as I held my breath dying to find out what Madison had concocted this time. Moments later, I heard the sound of soft hands caressing someone's thighs and a woman purring.

*Good*, I thought, pressing my hand back down over my dripping mound. At least there's another girl involved. I couldn't place her voice yet, but I was excited to see if it was someone I knew.

"Your hands are so soft," the woman said. I cocked my head recognizing the timbre of her voice. "I like the way you're caressing my thighs."

I recognized the voice instantly. It was my sex therapist friend Hannah, who I'd had more than one sexy rendezvous with myself.

"Mmm," another woman's voice purred between her legs.

*Fuck yes*, I smiled, feeling my nipples hardening. *This is what I've been waiting for—hearing two women get it on.* I spread my thighs further apart, pressing my fingers against my twitching clit.

"Don't be shy," Hannah said to her hesitant partner. "Feel free to touch me in *other* places."

It seemed obvious that this was the first time her partner had touched another woman this way, and I felt a stream of juices run down the crack of my ass as my pussy twitched in excitement. With nobody else watching, I hoped that the new girl could be encouraged to explore Hannah's body more directly.

I heard the sound of the girl's hands moving further up Hannah's thighs, and she moaned softly.

"Yes," Hannah said. "Press your hands up against the side of my vulva. Can you feel the heat between my legs?"

"Mmm–mmm," the girl hummed.

"Is this your first time touching a woman this way?" Hannah said.

"Mmm–mmm," the girl nodded.

"Feel free to explore at your own pace," Hannah said. "There's no expectations or pressure here. It's just you and me, and nobody else is watching."

"Okay..." the younger woman's voice said.

"Hold your hand over my pussy to see how wet you've made me," Hannah instructed.

I heard the girl shift her body a little closer to Hannah's chair then the sound of wet skin being touched.

"Yes," Hannah moaned. "Your hand feels warm against my cunny. Caress my lips and probe deeper. That feels good."

"Mmm," the girl purred as I heard the smacking sounds grow louder.

"You're making me get all warm and puffy," Hannah sighed. "Can you feel how plump my lips are getting?"

"Yes..." the girl said.

"Press your finger inside me. I want you to see how tight and wet I am."

As I listened to the two women interacting, I suddenly became aware of how quiet the rest of the room had become while everybody strained to listen. Not wanting to interrupt the girls' rhythm, I circled my clit quietly with two fingers while I sat mesmerized on my chair.

Suddenly Hannah groaned as she pressed her body lower in her chair, taking the girl's finger deep inside her pussy.

"Oh God," she panted. "You have no idea what you're doing to me. I love feeling you inside me. Place another finger into my slit and curl your fingers toward the front of my pussy. I want to feel you caress my G-spot."

A few chairs around the room suddenly squeaked as some of the guests adjusted their position uncomfortably. It was obvious I wasn't the only one getting turned on listening to two girls touching each other–especially knowing that for one of them, it was her first lesbian experience.

"Fuck yes," Hannah panted. "Just like that. Can you feel my pussy squeezing your fingers while you caress me inside?"

"Mmm–hmm," the girl hummed shyly.

"That feels incredible the way you're stroking me. Can you see my clit pushing out of its hood?"

"Yes," the girl groaned, becoming aroused watching Hannah's splayed pussy mere inches in front of her face.

"Let me feel your breath on my pearl while you caress me."

"Okay..." the girl said, shifting closer to Hannah's dripping pussy.

"Mmm," Hannah purred. "I feel you so close to me now. Blow on my clit while I imagine you watching me."

I heard a soft blowing sound then Hannah groaned more loudly.

"Oh God," she said. "You're driving me insane. Can I feel your lips on me? Even if for just a brief kiss?"

I smiled at how Hannah was gently coaxing the girl to take progressively bolder steps exploring her body. She was an experienced therapist who'd had many years of experience bringing similarly uptight women out of their shells.

I heard the girl press her body slowly forward, followed by a wet smacking sound.

"Yes, baby," Hannah purred. "Take my jewel between your lips. Feel how hot and hard I am for you. Let me feel you suck my bean while I squeeze your fingers. Can you see what you're doing to me?"

"Mmm," the girl moaned into Hannah's pussy.

"Swirl your tongue over my button now," Hannah said, continuing to guide the girl. "Show me how a woman is properly made love to."

"*Fuckk*," Hannah groaned, gripping her chair's armrests tightly with her hands. "Your tongue feels so hot on my clit. Suck me harder into your mouth while you swirl your tongue in circles over my nub."

Suddenly, the familiar sound of squeaking chairs from around the circle filled the room as the rest of the group began to get more and more aroused listening to the two women. I thrust three fingers into my pussy and began pressing them in and out of my hole, trying to imagine what Hannah was feeling.

"Yes baby," she panted more deeply. "Now curl your fingers against the inside of my pussy while you suck and tease my clit. You're doing an amazing job. I haven't felt someone excite me like this in a long time."

I suspected Hannah was stretching the truth a little bit there, knowing how often the two of us had shared a passionate encounter, but I liked how she was continuing to give her partner positive encouragement.

"Are you enjoying this as much as I am?" she said to the girl.

"Mmm-hmm," the girl hummed in agreement.

"Do you want to make me come with your sweet mouth?"

"Mmm–hmm," she hummed even louder.

"Press your fingers deep inside me while you keep caressing the front of my pussy. Maintain the steady action of your tongue over my clit. Flick it from side to side, then roll your tongue over it in figure-eight motions. I want to feel you sucking my whole gland."

I heard the girl shift her weight to get more comfortable between Hannah's legs then Hannah uttered a deep guttural moan.

"Fuck *yes*, baby," she said. "Just like that. God damn, you sure know how to eat a girl's pussy. Suck my clit. I'm going to cum soon. I'm going to cum all over your sweet face."

For the next thirty seconds, all I could hear was the escalating sound of Hannah's breathing and the accelerated squeaking of her chair a few feet to my left. Every so often, I heard the soft moaning and grunting of other guests pleasuring themselves as they listened to the two girls, and I began to jerk my hand harder up against my snatch, feeling my own pleasure beginning to build.

"That's it, baby," Hannah hissed. "Don't stop. That's perfect. I'm going to come soon. Oh God...I'm cumming! *Nnngh!!*"

This time I managed to hold off coming long enough to listen to the sounds of pleasure emanating from all around me in the room. My pussy twitched while I listened to Hannah climaxing in her partner's mouth then the rest of the group coming one after another.

"I'm still cumming baby!" she panted. "Don't take your mouth off me. Can you feel me pulsing on your fingers?"

"Mmm," the girl moaned, thoroughly enjoying how well she'd managed to please her partner.

"*Uhnn, uhnn, uhnn,*" Hannah grunted with each powerful contraction of her pussy.

It seemed to take almost a full minute for her to stop thrashing in her chair before silence filled the room once again.

"Whoever you are," she sighed after finally coming down

from her climax. "You're a quick learner. That was amazing. Come up here and kiss me. I want to thank you properly for your amazing performance."

The girl lifted herself up off the carpet and pressed her body closer to Hannah then I heard the sound of the two women kissing.

"Come sit on my lap, baby," Hannah said after a few moments. I want to feel your tits pressing up against me."

I heard Hannah's chair squeak as the girl placed her legs through the open armrests and sat down spread-eagled on her lap.

"Your body feels so hot against my skin," Hannah said, kissing her face softly. "Your tits are nice and full. And your nipples are hard. Do you like it when I squeeze them like this?"

"Yes," the girl panted.

I heard the sound of Hannah's hands roaming over the girl's body, then the familiar sound of someone's fingers pressing into a moist pussy.

"How about *this*?" Hannah said. "Do you like it when I touch you *here*?"

"Fuck, yes," the girl panted.

"Ahem," Madison said, clearing her throat. "Don't forget the rules. This is supposed to be a *one-way* engagement only."

"But she's obviously enjoying this," Hannah protested. "And since it's her first time with another woman, can't we make an exception?"

"She'll have her chance soon enough," Madison said. "If you two can't control yourselves, perhaps it's time to separate..."

"Wait," Hannah said as the girl began to lift herself from the chair. "I'd like to try one more thing. Can you change your position so you're facing the other way, with one of your legs threaded through one side of the armrests? That way we'll be able to touch our pussies together and I can enjoy this connection in a *different* way. That's allowed, right Madison?"

"As long as your partner will be able to contain herself," she said. "But I have my doubts. I'd hate to see her miss out on her own one-on-one opportunity later tonight."

"Just try it for a few seconds," Hannah said to the girl. "I want you to get a taste for what it feels like when two women join together in the most intimate way. Don't worry about making me come again if you find it too hard to continue. Let's just have a little fun together."

"I like the sound of that," the girl said. "But you might have to show me how to position my body correctly. I've never done it like this before."

"Stand up and turn your body around so your ass is facing my hips," Hannah instructed. "Then put your right leg through the armrest on the right side of my chair and sit down on my lap. I'll take care of the rest."

"Okay," the girl said.

I heard her shift her feet on the carpet then the squeaking sound of the chair as the girl sat down over Hannah's hips.

"That's it," Hannah said. "Now lean forward while I tilt my hips up. Can you feel the heat between my legs?"

"Yes," the girl panted.

"Just a couple more inches and–"

"*Uhnn!*" the girl suddenly groaned.

"Can you feel that baby? I'm touching my pussy against yours. Can you feel our wet skin joining together?"

"Oh God," the girl moaned. "That feels incredible. I never even imagined–"

"It only gets better," Hannah purred, grabbing the girl's hips, pulling her harder toward her snatch. "God, you're burning up against me."

"Yes," the girl groaned. "Fuck me with your pussy. Rub your cunt against mine. I want to feel *every* part of you rubbing up against me."

"Mmm," Hannah moaned, as her chair began to squeak rhythmically.

"Does that feel good, baby?" she said.

"Fuck, yes," the girl moaned.

"Lean forward a bit more while I tilt my hips higher..."

"Nnngh," the girl groaned more loudly.

"Do you like that? Can you feel my clit rubbing up against yours?"

"Yes," the girl said. "Don't stop. That feels so good."

As I listened to the two women's breathing rate escalate toward the inevitable tipping point, I knew even before she said anything what was going to happen next.

"You have no idea how much I hate to do this," Madison interrupted again. "But I'm going to have to ask you two to slow down or separate. I don't think your partner is going to be able to hold out much longer."

"You are *so* cruel, Madison!" Hannah huffed. "How can you deny this beautiful creature her chance to enjoy her first lesbian experience to the fullest?"

"I promise I'll give her a chance to consummate the experience later. Why don't you finish up now so we can move on to the next couple? But I suggest you try a different position to avoid putting your partner over the edge."

"Jesus," Hannah said. "I was just about to come. What do you think, baby? Do you mind finishing me off another way then I'll try to make sure you're properly taken care of later?"

"I'll try," the girl said, still breathing heavily. "What do you want me to do?"

Hannah paused for a moment, contemplating the simplest way to get off, then she shifted her position in her chair.

"Can you lift yourself up a few inches and reach between my legs? I'd love to feel you finish me with your hands while I caress your body."

The girl straightened her legs and lifted her body off Hannah a few inches, then I heard her hand moving over Hannah's wet vulva as she began moaning in pleasure again.

"Yes, baby," Hannah said. "That's perfect. Rub your fingers in circles over my hard clit while I squeeze your tits. It won't take long to make me cum this time."

"Mmm," the girl purred as the chair began squeaking from the weight of her hand propping her body up on the side armrest.

"Your nipples are so hard," Hannah moaned. "Next time I want you to fuck me with your tits. I hope this won't be the last time we have a chance to be together."

"Absolutely," the girl said. "This is way better than fucking a man. They're only interested in one thing, and they're always in such a hurry to get it over with. I'm not sure I'll *ever* go back after this."

"That's my girl," Hannah purred. "I'm ready now. Press your fingers harder against my clit and move them around in circles over my shaft. I love the way you're touching me."

"Yes," the girl purred. "I want to feel you come in my hands. Spray your juices all over me."

"Oh *fuckk*!" Hannah suddenly howled, losing control hearing the girl talk dirty to her. "I'm cumming, baby. I'm cumming so hard. *Uhnnn*!"

Suddenly, I heard the whole room erupting in a cacophony of grunts and groans as the other men and women around the circle could no longer contain their pleasure listening to Hannah having another powerful climax. I'd been holding back for the big finish too, and as I listened to Hannah gushing all over the girl's ass perched inches above her flapping pussy, I grunted loudly as I sprayed my own juices all over my seat.

5
___________

**MM**

"Okay then," Madison said after giving Hannah a few moments to recover. "That certainly was exciting. Who'd like to give it a try next?"

I heard some chairs squeak as a few more guests put up their hands.

"I'm glad to see you're all enjoying this enough to want to participate directly. But I'd like to stretch everyone's horizons a bit this time and test some new combinations."

There was some shuffling sounds a few feet to my left, then a group of footfalls moved across the carpet to the other side of the circle.

"Allow me to escort the lady back to her chair to make sure nobody trips over each other. Now, let's see," Madison paused. "Yes—I think *this* might make for an interesting pairing."

I heard some heavier footsteps being escorted to the opposite side of the circle, then Madison sat back down in her chair.

"Remember," she instructed, "there's no pressure to do anything you don't want to do. That applies to both of you.

But you never know how much you might enjoy something until you try it. So I encourage both of you to explore each other at your own pace and open your minds to some new possibilities."

*Hmm*, I thought, rubbing my slippery thighs together. *This sounds even more interesting than the last two pairings. What has Madison cooked up this time?*

The room was quiet for a few moments, then I heard the sound of someone kneeling on the carpet in front of the designated chair. There was a brief scuffing noise that sounded like hands rubbing against hairy skin, then it stopped almost as abruptly.

The room filled with awkward silence for a few moments, then Madison interjected to break the tension.

"I can see both of you are feeling a little squeamish. Remember, this is all about sharing new experiences and enjoying the attention of different partners without any judgment or preconceptions. I encourage both of you to open yourselves up to try something new. *All* of us have fantasized about exploring new sexual boundaries at one time or another. This is one place where it's completely safe and judgment-free. Am I right, ladies and gentlemen?"

A soft cheer rose from around the circle as the guests clapped quietly.

"See?" Madison said. "Nobody here cares who's connecting with whom, and they'll never know anyway unless you choose to reveal it later. Live in the moment and enjoy yourselves for a while!"

There was another awkward silence then I heard the squeak of a chair and the crinkling of plastic as someone spread their legs further apart. The other person hesitated for another long moment, then I heard the sound of hands moving over rough skin.

*Okay*, I nodded. *That definitely sounds like a man's thighs this time, unless someone hasn't shaved her legs in quite a while. The only question now is, is his partner a man or a woman?*

The scratching sound seemed to get rougher and rougher until I heard the familiar sound of skin rubbing over stubble.

*There we go*, I smiled. *At least someone's done some grooming down there.* I could almost see the man's cock slowly inflating as his partner caressed his bristly pubis and private parts.

"Uhnn," a husky-sounding man groaned, shifting his position again in his chair. "That feels good, whoever you are. You're making me hard."

I heard his partner exhale deeply and wondered if it was because they were getting turned on watching the man get aroused or because they were nervous about proceeding.

"If you just want to touch me with your hands, that's cool," the man said, sensing his partner's hesitation. "I've never done it with a man before, but so far it feels just as good as with any woman I've been with."

*So it's an all-male coupling this time*, I nodded excitedly. I'd always been fascinated watching gay men have sex online, and the thought of two *straight* guys hooking up excited me even more. I spread my legs apart and began stroking the sides of my vulva, trying to imagine what he was feeling.

"Yeah, play with my balls, man," the receiving man groaned. "That feels good. I can never get my girlfriend to give me enough attention down there. They always think it's all about the cock."

"Mmm," his partner hummed in agreement.

*Fuck, this is hot*, I thought, feeling my juices begin to run down over my slit. Listening to two guys who knew what they liked was utterly fascinating. I wondered how many straight women around the room were making mental notes of how to better please their partners, just like the *guys* were when Hannah and her partner were getting it on.

"Fuck man," the husky-voied man purred. "I'm hard as a rock. My dick is flapping up against my stomach. Grab my shaft and feel how hard I am."

"Uhnn," the other man grunted, his breathing beginning to grow more ragged.

Straight or not, it was apparent he was getting just as excited as his partner feeling another man's hard cock in his hands. I suddenly wished I could lift my blindfold again to see his lengthening cock swinging between his legs while he leaned over to touch his partner. The scene was becoming more exciting by the moment.

"Yeah, man," the first man groaned. "Grab me with two hands. Squeeze my shaft while you stroke me up and down."

As I strained to listen, all I could hear was the sound of both men breathing heavily.

"Fuck, yes, that feels so good. Can you feel my head popping in and out of your hands while you stroke me?"

"Uh–huh," the other man nodded.

"I'm getting sticky on top with precum. Do you mind putting some lube on my dick to make it more slippery? I want to enjoy this handjob properly."

I heard a tapping sound as the other man reached over to the side table, then a pop as he flipped open the lid and squirted some lube over the top of the other man's cock. Seconds later, I heard the familiar slapping sound of skin rubbing against wet skin as the first man began to moan louder.

"Yeah, man," he groaned. "That's so much better. Squeeze me hard while I pump my cock in your hands. Are you getting hard too?"

"Uhnn," the other man grunted, which I took to be a yes. Now I *really* wanted to take my blindfold off to see the two of them getting aroused touching each other.

"God damn, that feels good," the first man moaned. "I like your tight grip on my dick. Can you feel my cum dripping out of the tip and down over your hands?"

"Yeah," the other man spoke for the first time.

I couldn't place either person's voice, but that didn't stop me from enjoying the experience to the fullest. While I listened to both of them grunting and breathing heavily, I circled my clit and moaned softly along with them.

"Play with my balls again," the first man said. "Squeeze them with one hand while you work the head of my dick with the other. Yeah–that's it, squeeze them tighter. Is that the way you like it too?"

"Uh-huh," the other man groaned.

"Listen," the first man said. "I could come any second now, but I'd love to feel your dick before I pop off. Can you stand up and let me touch it for a second? I've never felt another man's hard cock before either."

*This is fucking awesome*, I smiled, feeling my pussy twitch listening to the two straight men exploring each other's bodies. It's even better than I imagined. Madison must have known when she selected the guests what she had in mind, and I nodded in appreciation at her courage in pairing these two up. Nobody's ever a hundred percent straight. Sometimes they just need a safe place and the right opportunity to explore the other side of their sexuality.

I heard the other man rise up from his kneeling position then take a step forward. Suddenly he groaned, as his partner grasped his cock in front of his face.

"Damn, man," the husky-voiced man said. "That's a pretty impressive piece of equipment you've got there. It feels like you're circumcised like me. And you're dripping, too. Can you do me a favor and touch your cock against mine? Maybe we can *both* have a little fun if that's okay with Madison."

"No problem on my end," Madison chimed in. "As long as your partner doesn't get too carried away."

The other man knelt back down on the carpet as the first man shifted his weight forward on his chair. Then I heard the lube container flip open again while the second man squirted some on top of his own hard-on.

"Yeah, man," the first man said. "I've always wondered what this would feel like. Place the underside of your dick up against mine, then let me hold them together while we jerk our cocks together."

I heard some more shuffling sounds, followed by a rhythmic smacking noise while both men moaned together.

"That feels incredible having your dick rubbing against mine," the deep-voiced man groaned. "Your cock feels so hot. Is this feeling as good for you as it is for me?"

"Yeah," the other man grunted. Whether he was just being shy about revealing his identity or he didn't want to show how much he was enjoying his first man-on-man encounter was unclear.

But *I* was sure as hell enjoying it. And from the sounds of other men and women around the circle, so was every-body else.

*God damn*, Madison, I thought. *This idea was absolutely fucking brilliant. Not only are you giving everybody a chance to stretch their individual boundaries, you're also giving the rest of us a chance to live out our wildest fantasies listening in on the action.*

"Can you picture our cockheads rubbing together while I grip our shafts with two hands?" the first man said.

"Fuck yeah," the other man grunted.

"I wish I could see it too," the husky-sounding man said. "Maybe Madison will give me a chance to switch positions with you later."

"Maybe..." Madison grinned a few seats away.

"Damn, man. I can feel your *balls* rubbing up against mine too. This is even hotter than I thought it would be. I'm getting close, how about you?"

"Yeah," the other man panted.

"Okay guys," Madison suddenly interrupted. "As much as I'd love to watch the fireworks, I'm going to have to ask you to disengage. Let's focus primarily on stimulating the gentleman in the chair. As you said, your partner will have his chance for reciprocal action soon enough."

"I'm sorry, man," the first man said. "But I promise to make it up to you later. I love the feel of your cock in my hands. I can't wait to watch you spew all over my dick. Do you mind finishing me with your hands?"

"No worries, man," the second man said.

I smiled listening to the dynamic between the two men. If this was how straight guys spoke when they had sex with each other, I found it kind of amusing. There was none of the usual love-talk between regular gay men. For some reason, it was turning me on even *more* listening to them pretending to sound all macho.

I heard the second man shift his position a few inches further away from the chair, then the rhythmic, wet smacking sounds resumed.

"Fuck yeah, man," the first man said. "I can feel your sticky cum coating my dick. Your hands feel so warm around my cock. It won't take long now. Squeeze my balls while you stroke my dick. I'm going to cum hard in your hands."

"Do it, man," the second man spoke up, momentarily forgetting where he was. "This is so hot watching your dick flare in my hands. You seem to be getting even bigger the closer you get to popping off."

"Yeah man," the first man huffed. "I can feel it. I'm gonna cum any second now. Let me cum all over your chest."

Suddenly, I heard the second man shift his position again, and the husky-voiced man let out an unearthly groan.

"Oh my God," he grunted. "Yes, suck my dick into your mouth. Your lips feel so hot on my dick. I'm gonna cum, man. Oh fuck, I'm gonna cum so hard in your mouth."

"Um-hmm," the other man hummed, obviously ready to accept his load.

"Yeah, baby," the first man growled. "Here it comes. Squeeze my balls. Oh *fuckkkkk*!!"

As I listened to the man howl in ecstasy, I could picture him pouring his load into the other man's mouth. It must have felt incredibly exciting for the other man to feel him pulsing in his hands while his partner exploded in his mouth. Whether he was swallowing his cum or letting it drip out of the side of his mouth, I had no way of knowing. But from the sounds of all the other grunting men all around me, it was apparent he wasn't the *only* one spilling his load.

6

## FF

After the two men had their turn, I eagerly awaited Madison's next choice of partners. She once again asked for a show of hands, and when she took my hand and escorted me to the other side of the circle, my pussy throbbed in anticipation to see who she'd paired me with. When I knelt down in front of my partner's chair and placed my hands on her thighs, my heart pounded when I felt the smooth, soft skin of a woman.

It had been weeks since I'd felt another woman's body next to mine, and I smiled at the opportunity to give the mysterious guest some girl-on-girl attention. I still had no idea if she was straight, bi, or lesbian, but it hardly mattered. I was about to give her a sexual experience like nothing she'd ever experienced before.

At least nothing she'd experienced *blindfolded*.

Her breathing began to deepen when she felt my hands on her legs, and I slid them slowly up the outsides of her thighs until I reached her ass. I took a moment to caress the sides of her buttocks, squeezing her muscles as she reflexively contracted them into two tight globes. I still had no idea who I was touching, but one thing was for sure. She hardly had a stitch of fat on her body, and her ass must have been a magnificent thing to see from behind.

The woman still hadn't uttered a single word, not even a moan or a sigh, but I could hear her breathing rate beginning to escalate the further I pressed my hands upward. With my face so close to her pussy, it was tempting to move closer toward her genitals, but with her seeming to hold back, I decided to press further up her body to see if I could get her to open up. I pressed her knees gently apart and pushed my breasts into her gap as I slowly lifted my hands up the side of her stomach toward her chest. When I felt the curvature of her breasts, I cupped them with both hands and pressed my tits against her wet snatch. I smiled feeling the river of juices cascading over my skin, belying her attempt to pretend indifference.

*Damn*, I thought. *This is one uptight girl. This calls for some more aggressive action.*

I raised myself up from my kneeling position, then threaded each of my legs through the armrests on both sides of her chair and lowered my ass onto her steaming lap. Then I slowly leaned forward until I felt her hard nipples touching my own. Twisting my torso from side-to-side, I flicked her teats with my tips then pressed my tits hard against her as I tilted my sopping pussy toward her quivering stomach.

As I leaned in closer toward her, I turned my face toward the side of her head.

"Do you like what I'm doing so far?" I whispered into her ear.

"Uh-huh," she squeaked softly.

I smiled as I nibbled and sucked on her ear, feeling her hot breath pulsing against my neck. Then I pulled back a few inches and squeezed her firm breasts, kneading her tips between my fingers. When she uttered a deep guttural growl, I leaned forward to kiss her. She pursed her lips, resisting my intrusion at first, and I bit her lower lip gently, sliding my wet tongue under the rim. When she parted her lips unconsciously, I thrust my tongue into her cavity, pressing my face hard against hers.

With my tongue probing her insides and my hands pinching her nipples, she slowly began to surrender herself as she tilted her hips upward, pressing her mound against mine. When she began moaning in my mouth, I grabbed both sides of her head, pulling her harder toward me. She responded by swirling her tongue around mine while rocking her hips, trying to increase the stimulation between her legs.

After a few seconds, I pulled back and smiled at the woman, sensing she was ready for the next stage in my exploration.

"Would you like me to move a little *lower* now?" I asked.

"Yes," she panted.

She still hadn't said enough for me to place her voice, but not knowing who it was turned me on even more. There was something about the idea of intimately touching a stranger–especially a straight woman–that I found insanely exciting.

I pulled my legs out from between the armrests and kneeled back down onto the carpet between her legs, determined to draw her further out of her shell. This time, as I pressed my hands up the insides of her thighs, I found them coated with a slippery film while she parted her legs, inviting me to move closer. When I pressed my hands against the side of her dripping vulva, she groaned softly and placed her hands on top of my head, running her fingers through my hair.

"That feels good," she said softly.

I thought there was something in her voice that sounded familiar, and I moved my face closer to her pussy, encouraging her to provide more verbal feedback. Normally, I would have been inclined to tease her some more with my hands, but I could feel the heat emanating from her pussy and her juices running down over my fingers, and I leaned in to encircle her flaming nub between my lips. When I sucked her clit into my mouth and began rolling my tongue over her exposed bulb, she groaned deeply, pulling my head in harder toward her slit.

"Oh God," she groaned. "That feels so good. Lick my pussy with your tongue."

I paused for a second trying to place the voice, then it suddenly struck me. It was my married neighbor, Valerie, who'd invited me to a pool party a few weeks ago at her house on the opposite side of my yard. We'd ogled each other's bikini-clad bodies for much of the event, but neither of us felt comfortable making a move with her husband and friends milling so close nearby. I was amazed how tight and shapely her figure was for a mother of two teenagers, and I couldn't take my eyes off her shapely ass the whole time I was there. For a long time after, I spied on her whenever she went outside to swim in the pool, masturbating to orgasm many times, wishing I had the courage to approach her directly.

Knowing I finally had my sexy neighbor exactly where I wanted her drove me crazy with desire, and I grabbed her ass with both hands, pulling her pussy hard against my face as I flicked her hard pearl with my lips and tongue.

"Fuck yes," she panted, losing herself in the heat of the

moment. "Suck me into your mouth. Your lips feel so hot against my pussy."

"Mmm," I nodded, happily lapping up her juices as she rolled her hips over my face.

Her breathing beginning to quicken and become more ragged, and I knew it wouldn't be long before she came. Whether it was because I was doing such a good job eating her pussy or because she was excited feeling another woman's lips on her clit for the first time, I wasn't sure. All I knew was that I wanted to enjoy her orgasm to the fullest when the moment came.

I held the tips of two fingers against her widening hole, then I pressed them slowly inside her. She gasped when she felt me penetrate her, and as I began to curl my fingers forward caressing the front of her G-spot, she bunched her fingers into a fist, clutching my hair with two hands. While I swirled my wet tongue over her clit, she pulled my hair harder and harder as she unconsciously clenched her hands approaching the peak of her pleasure. When she finally hit the tipping point, she screamed out loud, jerking her hips hard against my face in spastic twitches.

While the walls of her pussy clamped down against my fingers in rhythmic pulses, I held my face against her vulva as I felt my own juices running down the insides of my thighs in sympathetic union. When her contractions finally began to subside, she loosened her grip on my hair, and I pulled away smelling the sweet musk between her legs.

"I'm sorry if I hurt you," she said. "It's just that I haven't felt a woman touch me like that and I guess I got a little carried away."

I wanted to tell her it was no bother, but she still hadn't guessed who I was, and I didn't want to spoil the mystery, so I simply nodded and mumbled *um-hmm* to indicate that I was fine. But I was far from being finished with my sexy neighbor. Before the evening was over, I wanted her to experience the full spectrum of girl-on-girl sex, and I had more plans for her. I leaned forward, pressing my breasts between her thighs, then I grabbed one of my tits and swiped it up and down over her slippery vulva.

"Oh my God," she panted. "Is that your–? Yes, fuck my pussy with your tits. You're so soft. Much softer than my–"

"Husband?" I purred.

"Yes," she said. "And slower and more sensuous. I love the way you tease me with *every* part of your body."

"I'm far from finished teasing you with the rest of my body," I purred.

When I felt Valerie's fingers reach down over her mound and begin to circle her clit above my breast, I reached out and stopped her with my hand.

"I think we might be able to find another way to stimulate you there," I smiled.

"Yes," she panted. "Rub my clit again. I want to come again."

I thrust my arms under her thighs and pulled her closer toward the edge of her chair, then I pushed her knees up toward her chest, placing my legs over the top of her armrests. Grasping the sides of her backrest for support, I lowered my pussy down on top of her flayed legs. When she felt my hot cunt press against her vulva, she groaned loudly in my ear.

"Do you like that, baby?" I said, mashing my tits against hers while rocking my hips against her dripping pussy.

"Fuck yes," she panted in my ear. Then she pulled my head closer to her face, breathing against my neck. "I know who are, Jade. I've fantasized about making love to you ever since you moved in next door. You're even sexier than I imagined. Rub your cunt against me. I want to feel you come against my lips."

"I'm not sure Madison's going to allow that," I whispered back. "But at least I'll be able to feel you coming against me. Until *next* time, that is."

"Oh, there's definitely going to be a next time," she panted.

"Hold on babe," I purred. "Cause I'm going to ride you like a bucking bronco."

As we began to rock our hips back and forth, the loud smacking sound of our two vulvas began to echo around the room, and I wondered how many of the guests knew just how tightly the two of us were pinned together. From the sound of all the moans and sighs around the circle, I guessed their imaginations were already wandering to some interesting places.

As Valerie and I pressed our bodies harder together, I reveled in the feeling of her hot, slippery skin rubbing up against my tits and pussy. It must have been a feast for Madison's eyes being able to watch both of our exposed pussies pushing over the edge of Valerie's chair as we gnashed our cunts together. While I tribbed my clit hard against Valerie's hard nub, we moaned in unison, feeling our passion rising in tandem.

"Hold on ladies," Madison interrupted, right on cue. "Are you going to be able to–"

"I *got* this Maddie," I said, holding out a finger from the side of my body. "Just give me one more minute."

"You're threading the needle here," she said. "I'd hate to stop you before your partner is fully satisfied."

I pulled my arms against the side of Valerie's back rest, drawing my face closer to her ear once again.

"Come all over my pussy, Valerie," I said. "I want to feel your cunt twitching when you come."

"Uhnnn," she groaned into my other ear as I felt a dribble leak out of her slit and down the crack of my ass.

"Yes, baby," I purred. "Come for momma. Grind your cunt against me while I feel you gush into my hole."

"Oh God..." Valerie suddenly grunted. "Yes, I'm coming! I'm going to cum so hard against your hot pussy. Here it comes. *Aieeeee!*"

Listening to Valerie scream in my ear as she clamped her pussy against mine in the throes of another powerful climax took all of my willpower to contain myself from coming along with her. But I knew from Madison's viewing angle that I wouldn't be able to hide my usual flood of waterworks. So I simply held Valerie close to me and purred into her ear, encouraging her to enjoy her orgasm to the fullest.

"Yes, baby," I said. "I feel your pussy pulsing against me. Come all over me, baby. I love feeling your sexy body against mine."

"Oh Christ," she panted. "I'm still coming. I'm still coming against your beautiful, hot pussy. *Uhnn, uhnn, uhnn...*"

I smiled, feeling the contractions of her vulva syncing with her loud grunts in my ear. I hadn't fucked another woman like this for a very long time, and I reveled in every twitch and groan of my newly liberated straight friend. Something told me this wouldn't be the last time we stole a few clandestine meetings away from the prying eyes of our nosy neighbors.

# 7

# FM

For the next hour and a half, Madison continued selecting random participants from around the circle until just about everybody had had a turn both ways. But I'd just had a single turn so far, and I was eagerly looking forward to my next pairing, especially since I'd been prevented from fully enjoying the last episode. But when she grabbed my hand and pulled me out of my chair, indicating that I'd be the giver not the receiver again, I paused and turned my face toward her inquisitively.

"But I thought–"

"Something tells me you'll enjoy being the one in charge of this next encounter," she smiled, leading me to the far side of the circle.

When I kneeled down in front of my partner's chair and placed my hands on their thighs, I hesitated when I felt the telltale bristly skin of a man. I usually preferred making love to women, but in this case I was prepared to make an exception. I'd been biding my time patiently touching myself listening to everybody else get off, but the tube of lube just wasn't cutting it for me any longer. I needed a proper, full-sized cock in my pussy to finish things off.

And besides, I thought. It would be kind of fun to explore a man's body while blindfolded, learning what turned him on without the benefit of any visual cues.

Not knowing the identity of the person she'd coupled me with, I decided I'd have a little fun teasing him with a slow build-up. I placed my hands on top of his legs and gradually slid them up toward his crotch, pressing my fingers into the inside of his thighs.

"Mmm," a husky-sounding voice purred. "This feels a little different than the last time."

My heart raced knowing it was the same deep-voiced man I'd heard earlier in the evening when he'd been paired with another guy. I was excited to feel his organ in my hands and give him a different perspective this time. Knowing he was straight, I suspected he preferred having sex with women, and I planned to give him an experience he wouldn't forget.

As I slowly spread his knees apart with my shoulders, I caressed the inside of his thighs with the tips of my breasts. I could feel his hairs standing on end while my hands slid over the goose bumps on his skin.

"Yes?" I purred. "Do you like feeling my tits against your thighs? Are you ready for a *woman's* touch this time?"

"*Fuck* yes," he panted, spreading his legs further apart.

"Mmm," I smiled, pressing my breasts up against his balls, feeling his cock already pointing straight up at full flagstaff. "Is there anything in particular you'd like me to do with my special endowments?"

"Yes," he moaned. "Rub your tits on my balls. Then tit-fuck me with those nice melons of yours."

I smiled at the crude labels men often used to describe women's lady parts, but it didn't bother me this time because I knew I'd be the one in the driver's seat controlling the action. And before our turn was over, I planned to make him *beg* me to do his bidding.

I grabbed the sides of my tits and lifted myself up a few inches, surrounding his cock in my cleavage. It was hard for me to tell just how big he was without touching him directly with my hands, but there was plenty of dick still poking out from the top of my tits even though I was bustier than most women.

"That feels incredible," he groaned, angling his hips upward, pressing his balls tightly against my chest. "Your tits are so soft and warm..."

"Softer and warmer than a man's hands?" I teased.

"Yes," he grunted. "I far prefer feeling a woman's skin against my body."

"You didn't seem to be complaining too much last time."

"Yeah well, when you're horny, just about anything will do the trick. But chicks turn me on a lot more than men."

"Well you better strap yourself in then," I said. "Because I plan to give you a hell of a ride."

Although I could feel his hard pole burning up between my compressed tits, it was hard to get traction rubbing dry skin on dry skin, so I leaned over toward his side table and grabbed the tube of lube, pouring a generous dollop over the head of his throbbing member.

"Yeah, baby," he said. "Lube me up. I want to fuck your tits and come all over your face."

*Fat chance of that*, I smiled. Apparently, he still needed to be shown who was in charge here.

I grabbed his dick hard with two hands and slowly

pulled them down the length of his shaft, coating his hard-on with the lube.

*Jesus*, I thought, feeling his thick phallus in my hands. This guy is the real deal. By the time my hands reached the base of his dick, I estimated he was at least nine inches in length. I wasn't even sure if it would fit inside me.

*I might need to change up my plan of attack after all.*

I wrapped my tits around his shaft, pressing them tightly against his organ, then I began to slide myself up and down his steaming erection.

"Yeah, baby," he moaned. "Fuck me with your tits. Feel my big pole sliding in and out of your pit. Stroke the whole length of my tool."

*He sure is full enough of himself*, I thought as I slid my breasts over his flagpole. *He knows he's got it and he likes to flaunt it.* But to be honest, I was digging it almost as much as he was. I enjoyed feeling a man's cock from time to time, and this one was far bigger than most.

I tilted my head up, hoping to get a glimpse of his head poking in and out of my slippery breasts, but Madison had tied my blindfold carefully enough to prevent even the slightest peek. As I listened to his dick slurping between my lubricated breasts, I felt the head of his pole poking up against the underside of my chin, and for a moment I was tempted to angle my face down and take him into my mouth.

"Oh God, baby," he groaned. "I want your mouth over my dick so bad. Can you suck the tip while you fuck me with your tits?"

I'd given enough blowjobs in my straight days to know how to satisfy a man, but I wasn't really into that anymore having long since shifted my preferences to women. And besides, I never much cared for the taste and texture of a man's cum, and I wasn't about to let him pop off in my mouth without warning.

On the other hand, I *did* want to drive him crazy with desire before I finished with him.

I pulled away from his beanstalk for a moment and leaned in, slowly licking him from the base of his pole to the flaring crown. I could taste his precum spilling out of his slit and dripping down his shaft while I continued licking him like a giant Popsicle. I was enjoying making him squirm, and I wanted to give him just enough of what he craved so that when we reached the end he'd explode with the biggest orgasm of his life.

"Mmm," I moaned, pretending to worship his giant phallus. "You're so big. I can feel every inch of your python with my tongue."

"Yeah, baby," he grunted. "Lick my dick like an ice cream cone. Make sure you swirl your tongue over the head to catch my drips."

Knowing his most sensitive part was the soft tissue under the ridge of his crown, I pointed my tongue and slowly circled my head around the edge of his rim.

"Oh my God, baby," he panted. "Yes, lick my head with your tongue. You know how to drive a man crazy..."

"As well as another *man*?" I smiled, feeling his dick pulse in my hands as two more drops of precum spilled over his helmet.

"Yes," he said. "Suck my cock, baby. I need you to swallow me. Let me feel my cock in your mouth."

I was prepared to give him a little bit of latitude, just enough to let him think he was still in control. But I had a plan, and it didn't involve him cumming in my mouth.

I lifted myself up a bit further, then I paused with my mouth poised over the tip of his cock. He could feel my hot breath on his cum-coated glans, and he pressed his hips upward, desperate to feel my lips around his shaft. I pursed my lips and emitted a long stream of spit that landed on top of his flaring head with a soft splat.

"Oh, fuck yes," he groaned. "Lube me up with your spit. I want to fuck your mouth so bad."

Feeling temporarily sorry for him, I lowered my mouth to his burning head and spread my lips, feeling his girth stretch me open until I had his full circumference inside me. I was shocked at how thick he was, and I gripped his shaft tightly with both hands to make sure he didn't press himself too much further into my mouth. As I began to bob up and down gently on his pole and swirl my tongue under his ridge, he placed his hands on my head and pushed down gently.

I was glad that I'd had the presence of mind to grip his dick hand-over-hand so there was only two inches or so at the top of his hard-on that he could comfortably insert into me. But that was plenty enough. With his coke-can-sized girth, my jaw soon became sore from being stretched so wide, and after a minute or two of sucking his tip, I pulled away to catch my breath.

"What's the matter, baby?" he said. "Am I too big for you?"

"You *are* pretty fucking huge," I panted, wiping his precum from the sides of my mouth. "Maybe you're better suited for a man's equipment after all."

"I'm sure there are *other* parts of you that can accommodate me more easily," he grinned. "If you can deliver a baby, I'm pretty sure you'll be able to fit my dick in your pussy."

"Maybe," I smiled. "But I'd like to have a little more fun playing with that thing first. I want to feel your joystick throbbing in my hands while I pleasure you. Would you like to see how a woman's handjob compares to a man's?"

"Absolutely," he snarled. "Let's see if your little hands can handle my big poker."

Chuckling at his arrogant attitude, I clasped his dick again with both hands and squeezed it as tightly as I could. He felt hard as a rock, and his manhood burned in my hands.

"Yeah, baby," he grunted. "Squeeze the cum out of my dick. Rub my shaft while I fuck your pretty little hands. Can you feel my cock throbbing?"

"Oh yes," I purred.

"Don't forget to play with my balls. It feels so much better when you stimulate every part of me down there."

I moved my right hand up to his crown then cupped his balls with my other hand, squeezing him tightly.

"Yeah, baby," he groaned. "Squeeze my balls. That feels awesome."

As I squeezed the tip of his cock with the fingers of my right hand, more precum oozed out the top, mingling with the lube, creating a loud smacking sound as the air pocket under his frenulum filled with the sticky mixture. I could hear the sound of other men from around the circle flapping their dicks as they imagined me giving them a similarly dedicated hand job. I was pretty sure every one of them fantasized about a naked woman kneeling in front of them, giving them every bit of her attention while she gazed admiringly at their manhood.

*Men are so predictable,* I thought. *They really are all about the cock after all.*

"Yeah, just like that, honey," the man grunted. "Work my head while you play with my balls. Do you want to feel me cum all over your tits?"

"Mmm," I said, pretending to play along. "Do you *want* to cum on my tits?"

"Yeah, baby," he hissed. "I just need a little longer, then I'm going to spray all over your pretty breasts."

Seeking to heighten his fantasy cum shot fantasy, I lowered my left hand below his balls, caressing the space between his testicles and his ass. I knew this was another sensitive space for most men, and one his previous partner hadn't explored.

"Yes," he hissed. "Tickle the area below my balls. That feels incredible. I'm getting close..."

"Knowing he was close to cumming and wanting to make him climax on my own terms, I slid my hand lower, pressing my little finger toward his pucker. When I rolled my digit over his sphincter, he groaned and pushed his body lower in the chair, pressing harder against me.

"Oh fuck, baby," he grunted. "Whatever you're doing, don't stop. I've never been touched there before. That feels incredible."

When I heard his breathing begin to escalate and felt his precum pour out of his slit over my hand massaging his head, I knew he was close to the point of no return. With a huge grin on my face, I pressed my little finger harder against his sphincter until it slipped inside.

"Fuck," the man moaned, angling his hips harder against my finger until it was buried two knuckles deep in his anus. "I'm going to cum baby. I'm going to cum all over you face. Fuck me with your finger–"

Suddenly I pulled my finger out of his butthole and pulled back, listening to his dick flap excitedly against his stomach.

"What the *fuck*, man?" the man groaned. "I was just about to come! What are you doing?"

"Don't worry, man," I said, imitating his macho-man language. "I have something even better in mind to finish you off with. You didn't think I was going to let you waste all that hard meat coming in my *hands*, did you?

"You mean–?"

"Yes, baby," I smiled. "I'm going to finish you with my pussy. Would you like to cum inside something a little warmer and wetter?"

"*Fuck*, yes," he growled. "Give me anything you've got. I need to cum so bad."

"Do you think you can hold off long enough for me to have a little fun first? With a weapon like that, I assume you've practiced firing it enough to learn how to properly satisfy a woman."

"I'll try," he said. "But maybe you should hold off stimulating me like that until you're ready. I don't know how much longer I'll be able to hold out."

"Never fear," I said, standing up and turning around with my back facing his chair. "I'll take care of it the rest of the way."

Knowing I'd just finished my period, I wasn't worried about protection. Besides, I wanted to feel his hot flesh inside me when he shot off his cannon. I grabbed his tool between my legs then slowly lowered my hips over his lap as I felt his mammoth organ spread me apart.

"Uhnnn," I groaned, feeling his dick sliding inside me.

"Fuck, baby," the man panted. "Your pussy is so tight. Fuck me with your pretty cunt. I'm going to cum so hard inside you."

"Yes, baby," I purred, flexing the muscles in my legs as I bobbed up and down on his pole, feeling his balls slapping up against my wet vulva.

As much as I wanted to squeeze his testicles rubbing up

against me, I didn't want to risk of setting him off. I'd planned this scenario pretty much from the moment Madison had planted me in front of him, and there was no way I was going to let him come before I'd enjoyed myself to the fullest.

The man grabbed the sides of my hips and began pistoning his cock harder inside me, and with his breathing becoming more ragged, I knew I didn't have much time left. I moved my right hand over my clit and began circling my nub furiously. The combination of his big dick filling me up together with my already heightened state of arousal from having him almost cum in my hands had already taken me close to the brink. As the two of us moaned louder and louder ramping up our rocking pace toward the inevitable climax, I suddenly heard Madison clear her throat.

I held up my hand in front of me, pointing it toward her like a traffic cop ordering a driver to stop. There was no way she was going to deny me this last chance to enjoy my orgasm while impaled on this beast of a man. Knowing we were the last pairing of the night, there was no need to save ourselves for anyone else. Signaling that I was ready to let him come, I reached between his legs with my other hand and squeezed his balls tightly.

"I'm ready, baby," I panted. "Let it rip. Let me feel you spray your firehose inside me. I'm going to cum with you."

"Fuck yes," he groaned, pulling my hips tighter over his cock. "I'm going to cum in your tight pussy. Here it comes, baby! *Ngahhh!*"

As the man emptied his gigantic load inside me, I clamped down hard over his dick, gushing like a waterfall all over his tight balls. Between the howling sound the two of us were making and the sound of my waterworks splashing over his testicles, it must have sounded like an erotic symphony for rest of the listening guests. While we wailed together in orgiastic union, I heard an orchestra of squeals and groans coming from all sides of the circle around me. I smiled in blissful delight, knowing that we'd provided a fitting finish to Madison's exciting blindfold game.

8

———

**GUESS WHO**

After the man and I recovered from our orgasms, Madison escorted me back to my seat. For a few moments, there was an uncomfortable silence in the room as everyone waited to see what would happen next. She'd mentioned at the beginning of the party that we'd have a chance to guess who we were paired with and that there would be prizes, but it was hard to imagine how we could do that blindfolded. With everybody sitting buck naked facing each other in a circle, the only question now was just how much we'd have to reveal.

"Well I don't know about you guys," Madison said. "But *I* certainly enjoyed this experience."

"Woo-hoo!" isolated cheers came from around the circle as everyone applauded loudly.

"Part of the fun in doing this of course," she said, "was in guessing who your partners were. I know for *some* of you, we stretched a few boundaries, and I'm really glad you opened yourselves up to a new type of sexual exploration. I hope we opened your eyes, figuratively speaking, to the myriad possibilities for sexual expression, even if it only allows you to better understand and appreciate the preferences of our LGBTQ brethren."

"Absolutely," one of the women hollered, with the rest of the group applauding even louder.

"So now, as we approach the end of our little parlor game, the question is–how comfortable do you all feel taking off your blindfolds and revealing yourselves in front of your fellow participants? I promised there'd be prizes for those of you who guessed correctly who your partners were, but we can only do this if we reveal our identities."

There was an awkward silence as Madison paused to let her comments sink in.

"I don't want to make anyone feel pressured to expose themselves to a bunch of strangers if you don't feel comfortable. So, if you'd like to exit now with your modesty intact, there will be no judgment, and I can escort you to the front of the house where you can get dressed and leave quietly. If so, please raise your hand now, and we'll allow you to make a graceful exit."

I cocked my head and listened to the telltale squeaking of seat plastic to see if anyone was raising their hand. But the room stayed pin-drop quiet as everyone held their breath waiting for the next step.

"Okay then," Madison said. "You're welcome to remove your blindfolds then and take a look around the room to see if you can find any clues as to who your partners were."

I pulled off my veil and swiveled my head slowly around the circle, smiling as I recognized a few familiar faces. In addition to Hannah, Valerie, and Lily, whose voices I'd recognized earlier, there were a few other familiar faces in the crowd. There were my friends Bonnie and Emma from last year's camping trip, Cheryl from my favorite sex shop in town, and my friends Dylan and Jake and from my previous job.

But at least half of the group were a mix of people I'd never seen before. As everybody crossed their arms and legs trying to cover up their naked bodies, a few of us chuckled when we recognized some of the obvious suspects. I was surprised to see even *Madison* completely naked, sitting erect in her chair with her firm breasts pointing proudly out from her chest.

"I see some of you know each other already," she said, "while many others are meeting for the first time. And yes, I've *also* been naked this whole time, enjoying the proceedings along with the rest of you. I didn't think it would be fair being the only one covered up, especially since I could see everybody else in the buff."

"Who are you *kidding*, Mad," I huffed. "You just wanted to have as much fun as the rest of us while you watched all of us getting down and dirty."

"You might be right about that," she smiled, being careful to conceal my identity among the other guests who didn't yet know me. "And enjoy it I *did*."

"So," she said. "Who'd like to go first guessing who your partners were?"

"Are we guessing as the *giver* or the *receiver*?" Hannah asked a few seats to my left.

"Both," Madison said. "There will be prizes for each correct guess."

"It might be easier if each of us said something first to help us place the voice," Cheryl suggested. "Or at least uncrossed their arms and legs to give us some more clues about their special endowments."

"Fair enough," Madison nodded. "But for those of you

who already know each other, I'm guessing you won't need too many extra clues."

Valerie was the first to raise her hand as she peered at me with a lopsided grin.

"Yes, ma'am," Madison said, giving her permission to proceed.

"Are we allowed to use names, or should we just *point* to our partners?" Valerie asked.

"That's between the two of you. Whatever makes you more comfortable."

Valerie lifted her arm and slowly pointed in my direction, making direct eye contact with me.

"I have to confess that I recognized Jade's voice while she was touching me. And I'd recognize those magnificent breasts anywhere. I've spied on her swimming in her pool from the other side of our yards for quite some time."

"Did you enjoy your first face-to-face, or should I say *body-to-body*, connection this evening?" Madison smiled.

"We'd met previously at a few neighborhood get-togethers, and this wasn't actually the first time we'd touched each other. But somehow it seemed even more exciting not being able to *see* her this time."

"I'm so glad you enjoyed the experience," Madison nodded. "What about when you had *your* turn to provide the stimulation? Do you recognize who that might have been?"

"Well it was obviously another woman," she blushed. "But I didn't recognize the voice."

"Would the recipient like to reveal herself, now that you've heard your partner's voice?"

Everybody sat quietly in their chairs, then Lily raised her hand, smiling shyly at Valerie.

"Ah yes," Madison smiled. "That was a memorable coupling, as I recall. Did you both enjoy your connection?"

"Oh yes," Lily purred. "Valerie has quite a way with her hands, not to mention her talented tongue."

"Well I'm glad you both enjoyed the encounter," Madison said, reaching beside her into a large canvas tote bag on the floor. "Because you answered one of your connections correctly, Valerie, I have a special prize for you."

She lifted a Pocket Rocket vibrator out of the bag and passed it down the circle toward her.

"I hope this little sex toy will keep you entertained on lonely nights when you think back on this experience."

Everybody cheered as Valerie took possession of the toy, pretending to rub it against her vulva.

"How about if we mix it up a bit now?" Madison said, looking around the circle. "Do any of the *men* want to try guessing their partners?"

Everyone paused for another long moment, then a muscular, hairy-chested man raised his hand slowly.

"Yes, Neil," Madison said, nodding in his direction.

"I *also* recognize Jade's voice now that she's spoken," he said, grinning at me sexily.

"As the giver or receiver?"

"Well actually, I think maybe she was one of the lucky ones who experienced it *both* ways we me."

"I think you might be right about that," Madison said, turning her head to smile in my direction. "She *did* break the rules, but we might have to give her a pass since it was the last coupling of the night. And what about your *other* partner, do you have any idea who that might be?"

He glanced around the room at the other men in the circle, pinching his eyebrows suspiciously. Then one of the men on the opposite side slowly parted his legs, gazing him in the eye. Neil glanced down at his swelling equipment and smiled.

"I can't be a hundred percent certain," he said, pointing at the other man. "But based on the size of the gentleman's cock, I'm guessing it might be him."

"What do you say, Ryan?" Madison said. "Do you recognize the gentleman's voice or anything else about him?"

"Ah, *yeah*," he said, glancing down at Neil's semi-tumescent monster. "That's not the *only* thing I recognize."

Everybody around the circle chuckled as they watched the two men's cocks beginning to swell again in recollection of their memorable connection.

"Well, Neil," Madison said, reaching into her prize bag again, this time pulling out a purple silicone ring toy. "For guessing the *lady* half of your equation, I'm passing around this lovely vibrating cock ring. Though I'm not entirely sure you'll be able to fit into it."

Then she reached behind her into a large duffel bag, pulling out a full-size inflatable doll. The round mouth had a large hole with a bright red ring of painted lipstick around it, and between the doll's legs was a large red slit.

"Maybe you'll be able to fit yourself more easily into this lovely inflatable companion?" Then she pulled another doll from the bag, this one with a puffy cock pointing up between its legs. "Or would you'd prefer to have the *male* doll?"

"I'll take the female one, thanks," he smiled as the rest of the group erupted in laughter.

For the next twenty minutes or so, Madison continued around the room until everybody had had a turn to guess and reveal their partners. Once again, she saved me for last, and I cocked my head smiling at her, guessing what she was cooking up.

"So I guess that just leaves Jade without a parting gift," she said. "Each of your partners have already revealed who you were paired with, so it doesn't seem fair to hand out two prizes. But because you've been such a sport saving yourself to the end this evening, I'll let you decide which prize you'd prefer."

She held up each of the inflatable dolls in her separate hands, looking at me with a devilish smile.

"You seemed to have an *equal* amount of fun with each of your partners," she smiled. "Something tells me you'd be able to entertain yourself for hours with either one of these dolls."

Then she reached into her bag and held up one of my favorite sex toys, the two-pronged Osé vibrator.

"Or perhaps you'd prefer this special toy which simulates the movement of *each* sex against your private parts?"

I peered at Madison through narrowed eyelids while I parted my legs slowly.

"*Actually*, Maddie," I said. "I've been thinking about a different kind of prize all evening. After everyone leaves, I'd like to have *you* all to myself."

"Why wait until everybody leaves?" she grinned. "Why don't we get it on right here and now where everybody can see?" She looked around the group and held out her hands, seeking input. "What do you say, guys–would you like to enjoy one last pairing without the restriction of the blindfolds?"

A loud cheer rose from the circle as everybody clapped loudly, egging us on.

"Which would you prefer this time?" Madison asked me. "To give or receive?"

"Fuck that idea," I said, lifting myself out of my chair and lying seductively on the plush carpet in the middle of the circle. "I want to fuck you every way possible. It's time you got some of your own medicine."

"With pleasure," she purred, crawling across the carpet in my direction.

As she moved toward me, I glanced around the circle and noticed many of the men had separated their legs, revealing their hard poles pointing straight up in their laps. Something told me this party was far from being over, and that before the end of the evening there'd be quite a few more connections made among the hot and still-horny guests...

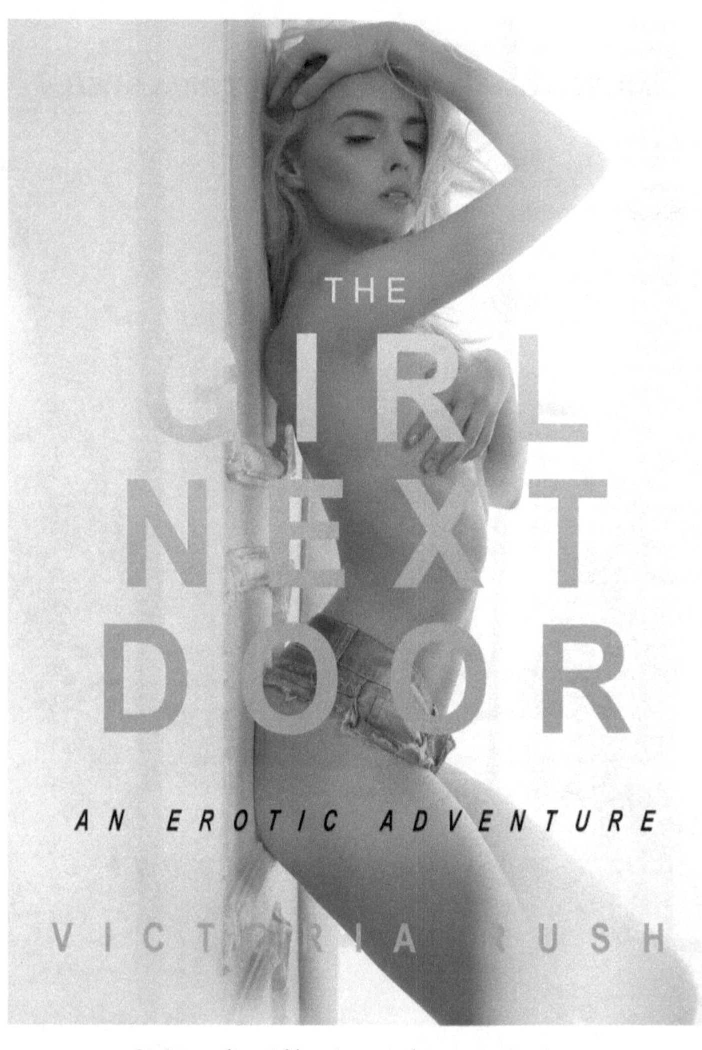


*Spying on the neighbors just got a lot more interesting...*

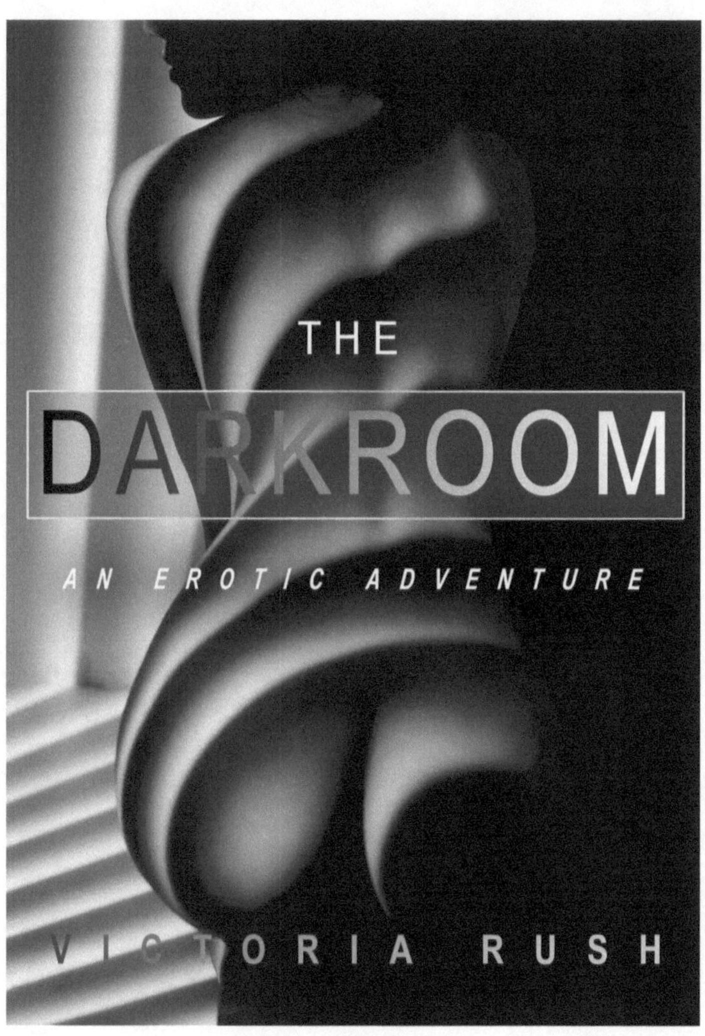


*Everything's sexier in the dark...*

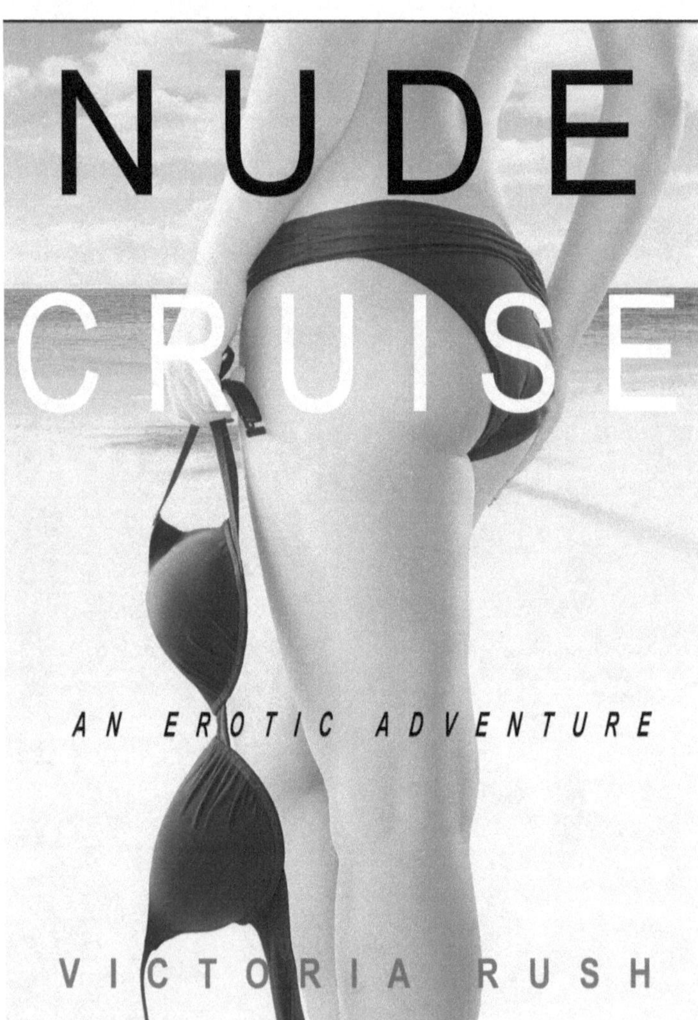


*Some people get wet on a cruise for different reasons...*

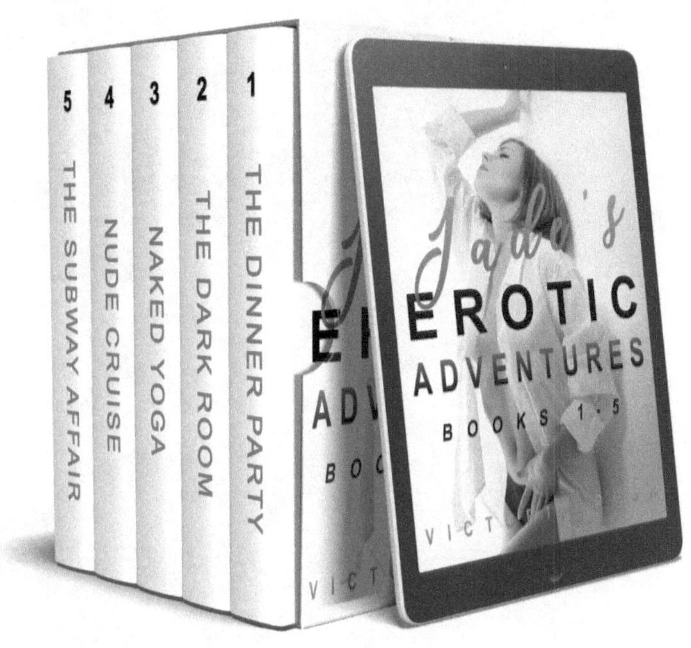


*Books 1 -5 in the bestselling erotica series - 60% off*

"Okay, so now that I'm committed, tell me where you had in mind for this little experiment."

"Actually," Hannah said, "I have a *series* of places in mind, each one more challenging than the one before."

"But I thought you said this was a one-off proposition?"

"I said nothing of the sort. I only said that if you won, I'd pay for the flights to Bora Bora. If you want me to cover the cost of hotels, food, and all the other incidentals, you'll have to pass progressively tougher tests. We don't want to make this *too* easy for you, do we?"

I crossed my arms and huffed, putting on my best pouty face.

"It hardly seems fair," I said. "But I'm still game. Besides, either one of us can pull out at any time to lock in our gains, right?"

"I suppose so," Hannah shrugged. "But what would be the fun in that? Something tells me once you've tried the first experiment, you won't want to stop. I think you're going to find this whole thing quite titillating and exciting. This will be the most fun either one of us has had in a long time."

I pushed the rest of my half-eaten salmon dish to the side, suddenly no longer interested in eating.

"Okay, lay it on me then. Where are you planning to take me for the first test?

Hannah gulped down the rest of her margarita then peered at me with a lopsided grin.

"Church. More specifically, a *Catholic* church. You haven't been in quite a while, have you? This will be your chance to repent and atone for all your sins."

"It's not like I've broken any commandments or anything–"

"The Catholic Church still considers sex outside of marriage a mortal sin. So technically, you've been doing a ton of sinning since your marriage ended."

"Well I haven't been a practicing Catholic for ages," I snorted. "So my conscience is clear. This'll be a cakewalk. All I have to do is sit quietly in my pew, right?"

"Yes, but it'll be a *front-row* pew, in full view of the priest who'll be delivering the sermon."

"Okay, but I'll be fully clothed, right? It's not like there'll be anything for him to see..."

"Not if you can keep your composure and don't cum all over the floor," Hannah said, cocking her head playfully.

"I don't think I'll have any difficulty keeping my dick in my pants, in a manner of speaking. But you raise a good point. You can't expect me not to get a little wet while you're stimulating me. What will I be allowed to wear?"

"I assume you'll dress appropriately, wearing your Sunday best. A mid-length skirt and button-up blouse should do the trick. You should be able to hide a few dribbles that way, right?"

"I suppose so, but how will we muffle the sound of the vibrator buzzing inside my panties? There's likely to be other people sitting around me in adjacent pews..."

"Never fear," Hannah smiled, reaching into her purse and pulling out a U-shaped silicone sex toy. "I've been talking with our friend at the local Babeland store. She's given me the latest prototype of the We-Vibe vibrator to test." She held up a smaller device with two control buttons and a flywheel. "Complete with a Bluetooth remote control. And the best thing is that it's whisper-quiet.

"Here," she said, handing me the flexible device. "See for yourself."

She tapped one of the buttons on the remote and the thick side of the contraption began buzzing softly in my hand.

"Okay," I nodded, looking around me to see if any other restaurant patrons were distracted by the gentle hum of the object. "It's *quiet* enough, but which end goes inside?"

"The bulbous end is a natural G-spot stimulator. You place the flatter end against your clit, then pull the thing up tight against your vulva to keep it snugly in place."

I suddenly became mindful of the wetness permeating my panties as I imagined the device vibrating inside me, surrounded by a bunch of oblivious bystanders.

"Can I give it a try here, like we did last time?" I grinned.

"No way," Hannah said, pulling the toy out of my hands. "There'll be no trial runs for this or any future tests. You'll just have to wait until we get to the church."

"And where will *you* be sitting while this is all going down?" I said.

"Right next to you, of course. I'll want a front-row seat to watch all the action."

---

On Sunday morning, Hannah picked me up and drove me the two miles to our local church. The entire time I squirmed in my seat trying to imagine what it would be like having a vibrator buzzing inside me in the quiet chapel. When we got to the church parking lot, she pulled into a sheltered space then plucked the blue vibrator out of her purse and handed it to me, resting her arm on the seat cushion expectantly.

"*What?*" I said. "You don't trust me to put it in privately?"

"Not really," she smirked. "For all I know, you might pull on some adult diapers under your skirt to hide any unintended releases. Here," she said, handing me a plastic vial. "I brought some lube to make it go in easier."

"I don't need any," I said, pulling the vibrator out of her hands and placing it under my skirt. "I'm already plenty worked up thinking about this scenario."

"I hope you're wearing panties under that skirt," Hannah said, watching me shift my weight as I placed the device against my vulva. "We wouldn't want it popping out at an inopportune moment."

"I'll just have to leave that up to your imagination," I sneered, lifting my skirt halfway up my thigh. "Unless you need to inspect the goods to make sure I'm not cheating."

"I trust you," Hannah smiled, opening her car door. "Something tells me you're looking forward to this just as much as I am."

As we approached the entrance to the church, I noticed a familiar figure standing at the top of the steps greeting the incoming parishioners, and he made eye contact with me when Hannah and I approached the landing.

"Jade!" Father Fife said, holding out his hands to me. "I haven't seen you in such a long time. It's so good to have you join us again."

"I'm sorry, Father," I said, placing my sweaty hand between his. "I've been a little distracted lately..."

"Life has a habit of getting in the way of the important things," he said. "We're just glad to have you whenever you can find time." He turned to Hannah, raising his eyebrows in curiosity. "And who's this lovely lady you've brought with you to attend our service today?"

"This is Hannah," I said, motioning toward my friend. "I thought I'd bring her along for moral support."

"Happy to have you, Hannah," Father Fife said, clasping Hannah's hands warmly. "The Lord knows we all need moral support wherever we can find it."

Hannah nodded politely, then the two of us walked through the entrance doors where I dipped my hand into the bowl of holy water and crossed my chest before continuing on toward the front of the chapel.

"*Jesus,*" Hannah whispered, peering around the imposing shrine. "Is it just me, or did that feel a little creepy? All that talk about *having* us and that prolonged hand-holding. Hasn't he been paying any attention to the me-too movement?"

"I'm not sure any of that applies to men of the *cloth,*" I chuckled. "But you better be careful about using the Lord's name like that around here. If anybody overhears you, you're liable to be burned at the stake."

The two of us stepped lively down the main aisle and finding a free spot in the front row, we took our seats flanked by two elderly couples. It was hard to imagine how Hannah would be able to use the remote-control device sandwiched so closely between other parishioners, and I crossed my legs, thankful for the brief respite. When everyone had filed into the chapel and the bell signaled the start of the service, a hush fell over the chamber and we all stood up as Father Fife walked onto the pulpit in his flowing robes.

"In the name of the Father, and of the Son, and of the Holy Spirit," he intoned solemnly.

"Amen," the congregation murmured in unison.

"The Lord be with you," he said.

"And with your spirit," the couples beside me retorted.

*What the hell have I gotten myself into?* I thought, feeling the flexible vibrator pressing against the inside of my closed legs. I didn't consider myself a terribly religious person, but being in this holy place surrounded by all the familiar rituals brought back all the old memories from my parents about the consequences of sinful behavior. *Surely getting secretly stimulated by a sex toy in the house of God will send me straight to hell.*

This was the point in the church service where every-body was supposed to take a moment to make a penitential act. While I listened to the other parishioners around me making their supplications, my knees began shaking as I made my own silent prayer for forgiveness.

"May Almighty God have mercy on us all," the priest said. "Forgive us our sins, and bring us to everlasting life."

"Amen," I joined in the congregation's response.

"Let us pray," Father Fife said, bowing his head.

As we closed our eyes and he began his opening prayer, Hannah nudged me with her knee and my mind raced with images of the pastor scornfully looking down at us while we played our blasphemous game. I peered up as he flapped his Bible closed, and caught him glancing in my direction.

"Through our Lord Jesus Christ, your Son," he said. "Who lives and reigns with you in the unity of the Holy Spirit, one God forever and ever."

"Amen," I said aloud, hoping he'd see me behaving like a good Catholic girl and turn his attention elsewhere.

He motioned for everyone to sit down and I was glad to get off my shaky feet onto the relative safety of the wooden pew.

"Good morning, ladies and gentlemen," he began his homily. "Today, I would like to talk with you about *morality*. Specifically, about the decaying state of society's morals in today's world. All around us we are surrounded by prurient symbols of modern decadence. First it was in the form of the printed word, then motion pictures, then the ubiquitous internet. It seems everywhere we turn, we are bombarded with profane and sacrilegious images."

I felt my heart pounding in my chest, like he was singling me out personally for my not-so-infrequent porn surfing.

"We seem to have forgotten," he railed, "the Lord's commandment that we shall not covet thy neighbor's wife. This admonition can be taken in its broadest context. Not only have many of you forsaken the sacred institution of marriage, but the egregious and widespread popularity of obscene *pornography* belies our unbridled lust and depravity. God slew Onan for spilling his seed, and so He will strike all others who practice self-abuse."

Hannah nudged her knee against mine, suddenly

reminding me why we were here. I was glad that she hadn't yet had the opportunity to take out her remote-control device, and I prayed that we'd be able to get through most of the service without her rudely interrupting it. I'd already begun to regret agreeing to this little venture, and I hoped that somehow we'd be able to bypass this first phase in her experiment.

"I'd like you to pick up your Bibles," Father Fife said, interrupting my thoughts. "And turn to Mark, Chapter 7, Verse 20."

Hannah and I reached down to pick up the bibles lying on the seat beside each of us, and we flipped to the indicated section.

"Read this passage with me, my friends," Father Fife instructed. "What comes *out* of a person is what defiles him," he enunciated, while the congregation quietly murmured along.

As I began to recite the passage along with him, I saw Hannah reach into her side pocket and place her closed hand between the book binding.

"For from within come evil thoughts," I continued reading as I peered out of the corner of my eye to see what she was up to.

"Sexual immorality, adultery, coveting, wickedness..." we read in unison.

Suddenly, I felt the interior end of the vibrator begin to tremble inside me and I stuttered, trying to finish the passage.

"Deceit...sensuality...envy..." I stammered, trying to catch my breath as I followed along. Hearing my labored recital, Hannah turned her head in my direction, acknowledging my silent suffering. She knew exactly what I was feeling and how difficult it was for me to remain composed as I read the script.

"All these evil things...come from *within*," I gulped as I began to feel the pleasure spread across my pelvic region. "And they defile a person."

"Consider these words carefully," the priest said, surveying my hunched-over posture. "For the Lord does not abide salacious thoughts and behavior. If you want passage into His Kingdom, you must be as pure and righteous as He."

He paused for a moment to let the message sink in, then he motioned with his two hands for us to be seated. I was grateful for the rest, and I froze upright in my chair trying to ignore the movement of the possessed instrument inside me.

"Let us consider for a moment *another* one of God's ten commandments," Father Fife continued. "Thou shall not commit *adultery*. The Lord made Eve from the flesh of Adam, and in so doing signified that forever more man shall be united to his wife as one..."

As Father Fife ramped up the intensity of his gayphobic critique, so did Hannah, furtively adjusting the flywheel on the remote-control device nestled under her palm in her lap. As she slowly increased the speed of the vibrations emanating inside my pussy, I squirmed on the bench, trying to restrain my rising passion.

"By rejecting the sanctity of marriage," Father Fife continued, glancing distractedly in my direction, "you have all *sinned*. In the book of Deuteronomy, we saw that God ordered adulterers be stoned to death. For your indiscriminate behavior, so shall the Lord indiscriminately smite thee."

*Jesus*, I thought. If that's what awaits a sinner for

cheating on their spouse, I wonder what happens to someone who self-abuses herself while sitting for Sunday Service in a house of God. *Surely I'll burn in hell for this act of sacrilege.*

Just when I thought I was beginning to get control over the delicious sensations stimulating my insides, Father Fife instructed us to stand once again and recite another passage from the Bible.

"Please stand now and read Peter 1:16 with me," he said.

Everyone stood and dutifully flipped to the relevant section of the scriptures. This time it was even harder for me to stand motionless, as my knees fluttered unsteadily from the pleasurable sensations radiating inside me.

"It is written..." I tried to read along. "That you shall be holy, for I am holy."

I saw Hannah's hands moving once again inside her prayer book, and suddenly I felt the *other* end of the U-shaped vibrator buzzing against my clit.

"And now Galatians 5:16," Father Fife instructed, barely giving me a chance to recover.

I flipped to the new citation and gasped for breath as my legs wobbled beneath me.

"But I say," I panted unsteadily. "Walk by the Spirit, and you will not gratify the desires of the flesh."

"So it is written," Father Fife said, closing his Bible. "Be righteous as the Lord, and you shall join him in Heaven for everlasting days. And now," he said, magnifying my torture. "I would like us to sing together one of my favorite hymns celebrating His blessing, *Amazing Grace*. Please pick up your hymn books and turn to page forty-three."

"Amazing grace, how sweet the sound," the priest began to sing as the entire congregation joined him in harmony.

"That saved a wretch like me," I sang along, trying to

ignore the message that seemed targeted directly at me. As I tried to hold the melody, Hannah cupped the remote-control device in her hand and turned the flywheel to its maximum setting.

"I once was lost, but now am found," I hyperventilated, pressing my legs together as hard as I could to stifle the rising passion that threatened to overtake me.

"Was blind, but now I see," I squealed, singing the last word decidedly off-pitch as Father Fife turned to see my entire body shaking as I belted the famous hymn.

By the time I'd finished the song, I'd somehow managed to keep it together and fight off the cresting passion that had threatened to put me over the edge. When we finally sat back down, Hannah mercifully turned the vibrator off, and I spread my hands over my ruffled skirt to signal that I'd managed to keep myself composed.

When the service was over and we walked up the aisle behind the rest of the assembly to exit the church, I couldn't wait to get out of the building to wash myself off, figuratively and literally. I was glad that we were at the back of the crowd so nobody could see the back of my skirt. I wasn't sure if my leaking pussy had left a stain, but I sure as hell didn't want one of the parishioners pointing it out. When we finally exited the entrance doors, Father Fife turned to the two of us and smiled.

"I noticed you seemed a little more passionate than usual reciting today's passages, Jade" he said to me.

"Yes, Father," I said, shaking his hand unsteadily. "I felt truly embodied by the spirit."

"And *you*, Hannah," he nodded. "Did you enjoy today's service also?"

"Oh yes," she said. "It was the most moving sermon I've attended in a long time."

"I hope you'll both come again," Father Fife said to the two of us.

"I'm sure we *will*, Father," Hannah smiled as we continued down the steps.

*Like the second we get back home*, I thought to myself, dying to tear off my clothes and squirt all over Hannah's face while she ate out my still-dripping pussy.

### READ MORE...

# ABOUT THE AUTHOR

If you would like to receive notification of new book(s) in Jade's Erotic Adventures, follow me at http://bookbub.com/authors/victoria-rush.

If you have a moment, please post a brief review on my Amazon book page at viewbook.at/parlorgames . Even just a couple of sentences will help other readers find and enjoy this book as much as you hopefully did.

Follow, share, like, and comment at:

www.facebook.com/authorvictoriarush
www.pinterest.com/authorvictoriarush
www.twitter.com/authorvictoriarush
authorvictoriarush@outlook.com

Hope to see you again soon!